Post Road Promises

Editor: Heather Hummel, www.HeatherHummelAuthor.com

Cover Design: Nancy H. Ramsey

Post Road Promises

JIM RAMSEY

PathBinder Publishing

Charlottesville, VA

What people are saying about
Post Road Promises

"Jim Ramsey really knows his territory — The Greenwich of 1979, before the high walls and hedge funders, when the town still had rough edges, dark corners, and great local characters. *That* Greenwich is between these covers."

- Timothy Dumas, author of *Greentown: Murder and Mystery in Greenwich, America's Wealthiest Community*

"My younger days in Greenwich came back alive in vivid detail. If I had been a part of a story like this back in 1979, I would have made Lieutenant a lot sooner!"

- Lt. Tommy Keegan, GPD (Retired), GHS 1971

"A fascinating look at my hometown. It reminds me you still have to be able to meet everyone at their own level, whether at the Bruce Park Tavern or the Greenwich Country Club. A fabulous reflection of life in Greenwich. I loved every word."

- David Theis, Greenwich Board of Selectmen, GHS 1967

Dedication

To Alex and Jennifer—

Achieving a goal starts with making a promise.

Acknowledgments

The author's name is on the cover, but a novel is a team effort. I offer my sincere and heartfelt thanks to my friend Mark, who lit a fire within me to develop these characters; to my skilled editor Heather, who could go over a fine-tooth comb with a fine-tooth comb and find room for improvement; and to my sweet and wonderful wife Nancy, who provided endless encouragement and support, and yes, designed the cover, too!

I express deep appreciation to the staff at Lake Wylie (SC) Public Library for their hospitality and to the Greenwich (CT) High School Class of 1971 for their memories and verification of era-specific details.

To my former co-workers at the defunct newspaper *The Gazette* in Greenwich, my classmates and teachers at The Greenwich Country Day School, and my friends during the 1970s and 1980s, — I thought of many of you while writing, and it made for a much better story, I promise.

Thank you! - *Jim*

Chapter One

Patty Callahan seemed unaware that several men from the weight room were watching her shimmy out of her wet bathing suit in her hometown YMCA. The striking blonde was a recent graduate of the University of Connecticut, where she completed a double major in Finance and Psychology. In no rush to join the hustle and bustle of corporate life, she was taking a year to weigh her career options. Sure, she had offers and leads from the financial sector in New York on Wall Street, but instead she chose Mason Street. The manager at the Putnam Bank & Trust on Mason Street took one look at her and her resume, and quickly added her to the staff of bank tellers with the possibility of doing more complex financial assignments. To stay close to one of her life passions, swimming, she also worked part-time as a lifeguard at the YMCA across the street. She put twelve years of competitive swimming experience to good use there. On several occasions, she had rescued swimmers in distress, and been duly rewarded by the United Way for her heroism with a small plastic plaque and a ten-dollar gift certificate to a local variety store.

In addition to having aquatic and diplomatic skills, Patty was blessed by Mother Nature. Her stunning figure was the subject of fantasy and gossip by the nearly two thousand male members of the Greenwich YMCA, talk she blissfully ignored. She had dealt with rude stares, comments and innuendo since she sprouted in middle school, and she had a repertoire of retorts and rejoinders she used with good effect. "Take a Polaroid, it will last longer," was one of her favorites. She had a bright and bubbly personality, but when diplomacy failed her, a fake-flirty look that quickly converted into a deathly serious glare or even the bluff of a quick slap in the face made her point in no uncertain terms: *You can look, but you better not touch.*

The YMCA Building Supervisor's responsibilities included a final check before locking up at closing time, something Mark Langford had committed to autopilot several years earlier. That duty required a ring full of keys for the fifty-odd doors in the building that needed to be secured every night. One of the keys was a small, shiny brass thing that had "P4" stamped on it. Nobody really knew what "P4" stood for, but the Supervisors knew the surprise it guarded inside an otherwise innocuous storage room.

About ten years earlier a new women's locker room was built just off the pool, and some vacant space upstairs was converted to a storage room to hold buoys, kickboards, and other pool-related equipment. To save money, instead of building a permanent floor the contractors built a sturdy perimeter walkway with lighter crisscrossing catwalks. All the equipment was stashed on shelves along that perimeter walkway. Every Building Supervisor was instructed to use extra care when traversing the catwalks, which were not designed to support more than one person at a time. That was a concern when bodybuilders found it necessary to be in a pool equipment storage room, and that night was no exception.

Mark was the only one of the four rotating Building Supervisors who had turned the "P4" room into a side business on the nights Patty worked. The day shift YMCA management knew Mark as a reliable and trustworthy employee, but his evening clientele knew him as an entrepreneur with a strict set of rules, secrecy, and financial arrangements.

Finishing his nightly rounds, he closed the pool doors then called the weight room on a scratchy-sounding but effective intercom system.

"Attention weight room. Drop and give me twenty," he said, but it was not a demand to do push-ups.

Several sweaty men poured out of the weight room, fishing twenty-dollar bills from their gym bags and pockets. Mark quickly inspected the basketball court with its suspended overhead running track and the Business Men's Club before hustling upstairs where they were waiting.

"Welcome back my friends to the show that never ends, we're so glad you could attend," Mark said. Some of them caught the rock and roll lyric, but Tommy evidently paid more attention to Joe Weider's muscle magazines than to *Rolling Stone*. He looked blankly at Mark.

"Emerson, Lake and Palmer," Mark explained.

"Who?"

"No, that's Daltrey and Townshend, you know, 'Who are you?'"

"I'm Tommy."

Mark sighed, but realized he now had an audience. The other guys smirked at each other and let it play out.

"Tommy, are you a pinball wizard?"

"What?"

"Do you like pinball, you know, the game?"

"No, just weights."

"But, do you have such a supple wrist?"

"For wrists I do z-bar forearm curls, dude."

"Okay, Tommy, that's good."

"So, Emerson and, ah… are those new chicks?"

"No, man, they're a band, you know, 'Come and see the show.'"

"Come and see the show?"

"Yes."

"I'm here for the show, just like you said. I got my twenty."

"Good, Tommy."

"Is Patty here?"

"Yes, let's go."

Mark produced the "P4" key with a flourish, opened the door, and gestured to the perimeter walkway. Tommy went in first. The other guys smiled and some patted Mark on the back as they filed in.

"That might have been worth the price of admission right there," one of them said as he brushed by Mark. He closed the door behind them. They quietly knelt down and pried up several white ceiling tiles suspended above the women's locker room, holding them open barely an inch or so.

Two of the men had a side bet on whether they would actually see Patty naked. There was a winner and a loser, which was fine, but the loser chose that moment to pay up his new debt. He pulled his wallet out of his pocket and

went to hand over the money. Somehow, the bill slipped from between his fingers and sailed through the tiny opening in the ceiling tile. Patty was standing beneath them, toweling off after her shower. The ten-dollar bill wafted ever so gently downward, and landed vertically inside her bra on the bench. Alexander Hamilton's face stared at her sideways. She stared back. They all froze. Mark silently lowered his ceiling tile then made frantic gestures to the rest of the knuckleheads to do the same. In their last glimpse of Patty, she had picked up the bill, and her head had started to tilt upward. He made more crazy gestures for the guys to remain quiet. They all sat in deathly silence but heard nothing through the floor beneath them beside soft shuffling, and certainly no shouts of anger. Mark whispered to them to wait a minute then slowly walk out one at a time. The last to leave, he tiptoed out of the storage room and closed the door with a barely audible click behind him.

Twenty minutes later, Mark was sitting at the front desk, pretending to read the local newspaper, the *Greenwich Time*, when Patty walked up with a blended look of puzzlement and amusement on her face. He automatically handed her a pencil and a gray metal filing box that held all the staff's time cards. After she finished filling hers out, she pulled something from her jacket pocket and handed both back to him. He received her time card and a ten-dollar bill together. His mouth opened to speak, but she had already turned to walk out the front door, giving him a wave over her shoulder. She said, "Good night, Mark, see you tomorrow!" As she did, she looked back with a quick smile.

6

Mark made a promise to himself to never let that happen again. He was hyperventilating as the last member to leave the YMCA that night came out of the Business Men's Club. Steven Rollins, of course, it had to be Steven Rollins. He was a reporter for the *Greenwich Time,* and Mark had known him for about a year.

"Hey Mark, how's it going?" Steven said in his deep voice.

"Um, pretty good, man. How are you?"

"Not bad. Spring can't get here soon enough, though. Our softball team is still on track, right?"

"Yeah, as far as I know."

"What are you listening to these days?" Steven asked.

"Oh, there's so much disco now, so mostly old stuff, like Emerson, Lake & Palmer and The Who." Mark smiled as he cracked himself up a little bit. "But right now, I like Dire Straits, 'Sultans of Swing,' that's some good guitar playing."

"Yeah, I like that, too. I bet you're sick of that 'Y.M.C.A.' song, right?"

"Oh, man, puh-leeese."

"You mean to say, it's *not* fun to stay at the Y.M.C.A.?"

"Like I haven't heard that a thousand times," Mark said, with an exaggerated shudder.

"I know. Well, I gotta get going." As Steven turned to leave, he had one of those Columbo moments; he stopped dead in his tracks, raised his hand over his head, pivoted on the heel of his left loafer, and turned back to face Mark.

"Oh, by the way," he said, "I've been hearing some chatter about you using the Rendezvous Room for booze parties when the Y is closed. Some other stuff, too. Would you care to comment on that?"

"Would you care to comment on that?" Steven repeated.

Mark shifted his weight, and shifted his expression. It was a blunt and invasive question, but Steven felt he knew Mark well enough to ask it, even though he was a part of the YMCA's management.

Suddenly Mark went into Eddie Haskell mode. "Oh gee, I don't know anything about that, man," he said through a plastic smile. "I leave here and go directly home almost every night."

Steven saw through the sanitized denial, and knew that Mark was smart enough not to get himself in trouble, especially answering a point-blank question from a newspaper reporter. Mark knew that Steven knew, and Steven knew that Mark knew that Steven knew. Steven's wry smile conveyed all of this. Their history permitted all this mutual understanding to take place in a few seconds.

"Of course. Maybe I misunderstood what I overheard," Steven said. "That's not your style, right?" That led to another round of "I know that you know that I know."

He's just a big fish in a small pond, maybe using the back room for some card games, pot, and sports betting for side income, Steven thought.

Steven was more interested in trying to track something bigger, and figured Mark's story, whatever it was, was much lower down the totem pole. He found it amusing that Mark had the *Greenwich Time* on his desk.

"Well, drive safely. See you later."

Mark knew that was a bit of a jab also. Steven knew what Mark drove, and had heard him grousing about the local police and the stack of tickets he was piling onto his driving record. As easily as Steven had turned to face Mark, he continued his spin in the same direction, again pivoted on the heel of his left loafer, ducked his head under the vacuum compressor on the top of the door, and stepped out into the night.

Mark watched him leave, glanced sideways down the hallway then picked up the newspaper again. He knew Steven was a regular at the Y, and his activity varied with the seasons. He would come in occasionally to use the weight room, but just for basic fitness. He didn't socialize much with the regulars. His main interest was to play after-work pickup games of basketball during most of the winter. He was often the tallest player on the court, and opponents played rough to try to stop him. When he couldn't navigate freely under the basket, he adapted by creating space, then shooting and passing over smaller defenders. Because the custom was for the winning team to stay on the floor, that edge helped him hold court as long as he stayed motivated. He was someone who used an edge when he had one, either subtly or obviously.

They played softball together, too. The YMCA's team needed players last season when Mark asked Steven offhandedly if he played softball. They found out at the team's first practice at Bible Street Park. During batting practice, Steven had a moment where he was able to block out the teens shouting and swearing on the basketball court and the children laughing and shrieking on the playground, leaving him totally focused on the task at hand. He used his exceptional leverage and launched one ball so far over the outfielders' heads they didn't bother to chase it. Everyone just watched as it landed in the street, bounced over a green AMC Gremlin, and rolled into a weed-filled yard between a little boy sitting in his Big Wheel and an old man flicking ashes off his Chesterfield. The old man and little boy watched the ball hop off the cracked cement of their front steps as it came to a stop. They looked at each other then both turned and squinted at the distant batter. The boy put the ball in his lap and started pedaling to return it to the field. Back on the diamond, the players shook their heads, smiled, and a few started laughing. Mark looked back and forth between the backstop and the blue, wooden house and tried to gauge the distance like Jack Nicklaus's caddy.

"Oh hell yeah, man, he plays softball too," Mark announced.

"Hey, a broken clock is still right twice a day," Steven replied. He waited for the next pitch and hit it about four hundred feet... two hundred feet straight up, and two hundred feet straight down. It landed near the pitcher, who caught it on the bounce and teased him with a wide-eyed, palms-up shrug. Steven's moment of clear focus had left as easily as it had arrived, but he didn't mind.

"*F Troop* back to normal, sir," Steven said, laughing. The guys laughed some more. They liked his sense of humor. They also appreciated that he kept a cool and relaxed demeanor and buried his personality to fit in, allowing Mark room to shine. Mark appreciated that, and Steven picked up on that. It was part of the foundation of a friendly but complex relationship. Friendly because they got along well and shared a passion for rock and roll and softball, but complex because one of Mark's best friends was a man named Frank Castino who ran Bruce Park Tavern, a popular local watering hole.

Steven walked out of the YMCA and pulled up his collar against the cool breeze. His left middle finger was sore and swollen from jamming it in a basketball game. It was late at night in the middle of a week in early March. The NCAA basketball tournament was just underway, and he was thinking about the all-around skills of two taller players, Larry Bird of Indiana State and Magic Johnson of Michigan State. For him, March meant he was between seasons...basketball was growing stale, and the local fields were too muddy for softball. The local league would start in April, sometime around Easter. Still, he felt fortunate to have these activities to keep him busy when he wasn't working, which recently had extended past traditional business hours. That was the nature of working in the media. Breaking news and scheduled meetings weren't confined to nine to five, Monday through Friday. Sometimes he felt conflicted about that...his work certainly paid the bills and then some, but he enjoyed his free time as well, and something as simple as working a couple of hours after dinner was enough to throw a typical evening completely out of whack. Late night assignments covering meetings were a different thing altogether, and that did happen fairly often. Those meetings were sometimes exciting on a professional level, but they upset his routine and Steven was a meticulous man who enjoyed structure.

He was standing at the curb near the intersection of the Post Road and Mason Street waiting for the traffic light to change when a silver Datsun 280Z squealed its tires behind him to his left. He looked over his shoulder and watched as the car ripped a left turn out of the Putnam Bank & Trust driveway. He thought it was unusual for a car to be in the bank's parking lot so late in the evening. The Datsun came up to the intersection, took liberties with a yellow light, and whipped a tight right-hand turn in front of Steven. As he watched the car accelerate down the Post Road, he glanced down to notice its personalized license plate. That was not unusual since Connecticut was among the top ten states in the country for personalized plates, per capita. It turned into something of a hobby for him, looking at these six-space plates and trying to decipher their messages. Some were obvious and some were not. This one said 200IM.

He couldn't immediately figure it out because it was dark and he read the white-on-blue plate as 2001M. The car bolted down the Post Road. License plates, crossword puzzles, number sequences, word and letter patterns, puns...they all caught his eye and triggered his interest. For instance, he was amused that Western Junior High School was on Western Junior Highway.

Steven looked both ways, walked across the Post Road and stepped into White's Diner. The door jingled as he opened it, and he paused for a moment, allowing the cool air to rush into the warm Diner. He was nearly as tall as the doorway, although not nearly as wide, but in his dark blue L.L. Bean down jacket and with his hands on his hips, he filled the frame pretty well. He liked to do that once in a while...sometimes to make a grand entrance, and sometimes just to see what reaction it would get. The Diner was far from a "make a grand entrance" type of place. Instead, the reaction he received was a furrowed brow from an older man at a nearby booth who felt the chilly air, and a tilted-head smile from a waitress who knew him.

"Hello, Mr. Rollins," she said cheerfully before turning to get the cup of coffee he would drink without actually ordering it. He walked over to the last booth on the right, took off his jacket, grabbed the glass ashtray and put it on another table. He liked that particular booth because he was able to see the entire room and also look out the window at traffic or at the front of the YMCA.

Steven looked at the songs on display in the chrome tabletop jukebox, but did not flip through the other selections. The waitress swung by and dropped off his coffee. No cream, no sugar, one ice cube to bring the temperature down quicker.

"Why, Miss Baker, so good to see you again," he said, smiling, completing their traditional greeting.

"You bet, Big Guy."

While he waited for his coffee to cool a bit more, Steven gazed vacantly through the streaky window. Sparse late-night traffic rolled by. A black Chevy Camaro, barely visible at night if it were not for the streetlights, waited and rumbled at the red light. Loud music blared inside the closed windows. Steven knew this was Mark's car. He had seen it several times at softball, and had been in it a couple of times when sharing a ride to a game made more sense. Plus, he knew the Y was closing, or was closed already. The Camaro turned left and headed toward Byram, just a few miles away. Certainly not the 1,111 miles from Greenwich to Orlando, a fact Steven found amusing, and a destination he found appealing. He was thinking about central Florida when his waitress, Susie Baker, came over to refill his coffee.

"Susie, have you ever been to Florida?"

"Why, are you inviting me to go?"

"No, not today," he joked. "I was just wondering."

"I've been to the Bahamas a few times, but not Florida."

"It's the opposite for me. Florida a bunch, but not the Bahamas, or Bermuda, either. In fact, I've never been out of the country."

"Um, so what's up then?" she asked.

"Nothing special. I was just daydreaming."

"Daydreaming at night?"

"Yeah, something like that."

"Well, sweet daydreams then," she said. Susie pivoted on the heel of her left shoe and went to another table. As she did, she looked back with a quick smile.

After Steven finished his coffee, he put down his empty white porcelain cup and dug out his brown leather wallet. He fished out a couple of dollar bills but his sore finger flinched. One of the dollars slipped out of his grip, wafted ever so gently downward, and landed vertically inside the coffee cup on the table. George Washington's face stared at him sideways. He stared back and wondered about the odds of that happening again, randomly or even intentionally. *Triple digits for sure.* He moved the money from inside the cup to beneath it and grabbed his jacket.

15

"Bye 'Soos,' I'll be around," he said.

"I know you will," she replied.

They smiled at each other again just before he ducked through the doorway and walked outside. The song "Wake up Little Susie" started playing in his head. The Everly Brothers hit topped the Billboard chart when he was a little kid. *She was probably teased about it when she was younger,* he thought.

He turned left and walked up the sidewalk, headlong into a cold wind, toward his car in the grocery store parking lot next to the Y.

Isn't it odd how one seemingly random decision can have a chain reaction of unintended consequences?

Chapter Two

Mark was speeding from the YMCA to his home in the neighboring town of Banksville, New York. For more than six years, he took the same direct route up North Street. Officer Danny Heaton must have pulled him over a dozen times, and each time Mark had acted as if they'd never laid eyes on each other before. That night he was a little rattled by Patty's *de facto* admission that she was fully aware of his Peeping-Tom-for-a-price shenanigans, and even worse, he didn't know what she planned to do about it. He was confused by her reaction. It was like she knew but didn't care. It seemed she had the upper hand now and he was uncomfortable with that. He could lose his job over it.

He was lost in his thoughts of the various consequences of unemployment and had a heavier foot than usual on the gas pedal when he saw the bright flashing lights in his rear view mirror. It was too late to let up. The police car had been camped out in one Officer Heaton's favorite spots, in the driveway of Sam Bridge Nursery & Greenhouses, one of the few businesses on North Street. Next to the Ace of Diamonds playing card Mark had jammed into his dashboard, the speedometer indicated his Camaro was cruising at seventy-one miles per hour. The speed limit on

North Street was forty. Not surprisingly, Heaton had a big smile on his face as he approached the Camaro. Mark snapped the ashtray shut, even though the cigarette in it was only a Marlboro.

"Do you know why I stopped you tonight?" Officer Heaton asked.

Mark was tempted to tell him it was because he had a half-dozen illegal aliens in his trunk and had to return them to the work farm just over the state line in Banksville, but decided against it.

"Was I going too fast?" Mark inquired, returning his winning smile. He handed over his license and registration. Heaton shined his flashlight on them and frowned.

"I clocked you going seventy," he said. "I should impound your car and arrest you, but I'm feeling generous; this might only cost you a couple hundred bucks."

Mark had his spiel memorized. He mimed it with his lips as he spoke. Heaton furrowed his brow and said, "You sit tight; I'm going to call this in."

Heaton turned and disappeared behind his flashing red and blue lights. Mark flipped the radio back on to WNEW. Styx was belting out "Renegade," which was somehow appropriate at the moment. He was still stewing over his dilemma with Patty when Heaton sauntered back up. He stuck a ticket through the window, along with his license and registration.

"Okay, here's how it is: You get four bucks for every mile over the limit which works out to one-twenty. You can contest it, but with your driving record, the judge will suspend your license and could send you to the State Pen in Bridgeport. Pay it by the fifteenth of next month, or that's where you're headed."

Mark considered himself lucky to get off with the fine and hung his head.

"I promise I'll drive more carefully," he said. It was a promise Heaton had heard before.

"See that you do!" Heaton replied. The officer followed Mark all the way to the state line. Mark made a promise to himself he would cool it on the speeding. He used the extra driving time to try to formulate a Patty Plan, but he was unsuccessful.

It was late and he didn't want to disturb his parents. The twenty-five-year-old still lived at home with his folks. For the past four years, he had a serious relationship with an *au pair* in White Plains but it fizzled out. His plan to spend a winter back at home to recoup carried into the spring. His father was the caretaker of a sprawling Banksville estate. The old maple door groaned on its hinges and a dull nightlight lit part of the entrance hallway. On the small antique table where the telephone was perched on top of a decorative lace doily, there was a note written in his mother's careful script:

"You had two calls," it said. "The first one was from a girl named Patty Callahan." When he read that he sagged like a moose taking both barrels of a shotgun. "She seems very nice, and said she would see you the next time you both worked at the Y. The second call was from a man named Steven Rollins. He said he was a reporter for the *Greenwich Time* and would like to buy you lunch. Here are their numbers..." Now he felt like the moose had not just been shot but skinned and mounted over a fireplace.

Mark liked Steven but thought he was an oddity. The Greenwich native attended the University of Missouri's School of Journalism and racked up several awards there, one of which was for an investigative report about Vietnam draft irregularities. He'd written for *The New York Times* and the *Hartford (CT) Courant* right out of college, but now he was back in Greenwich, excelling by doing investigations, such as a big theft of medical supplies at Greenwich Hospital and budget overruns in the town's snow removal budget. He could ferret out wasteful expenditures by the town government like nobody's business. Mark saw him frequently at the Y, but knew him better through their softball team. He seemed affable enough, and recently was angling for some face time. The only thing he could figure was that Steven had heard about his Sergeant Bilko routine and wanted the sordid details. Mark felt pretty confident that he ran a tight operation. He was more concerned about Patty; she was no dummy. She could do quadratic equations in her head and had smooth-talked her way out of many sticky situations with men at the Y. Because she was a sharp girl with a finance degree, the bank manager frequently gave her special assignments. She was learning to use the bank's computer, which was linked to a state-of-the-art IBM "System/370" with a "Multiple Virtual Storage" operating system in IBM's inter-modem relay center in nearby Purchase, New York. It didn't take her long to acclimate to the system, to learn her way around its features and options, and to access the files within the bank. She could complete her assignments, and frequently came up with extra findings and recommendations, which impressed the manager and led to more complex tasks and the likelihood of being promoted to Assistant Manager.

Mark trudged up the stairs to his small room and turned on the small TV; Johnny Carson was enjoying listening to some of the cast members of the old *F Troop* comedy series. Forrest Tucker was telling a behind-the-scenes story about sneaking real whiskey into the saloon in town for a scene being shot there. His character, Sergeant O'Rourke, secretly ran the saloon behind the back of the Captain and the Army. Tucker said several cast members enjoyed that scene a bit too much and they had to cancel the rest of the day's schedule. The crowd roared, Ed McMahon guffawed and Johnny giggled and pitched to a commercial break. "We'll be right back." Mark dozed off before Johnny's next segment, so he missed seeing Marlon Perkins's African Ring-Necked Parakeet get loose and fly around the set before landing on Johnny's shoulder.

Chapter Three

Steven's house was a functional place, but pretty nice. It was certainly above his pay-grade. He hardly ever talked about it because there was no way a newspaper writer could normally afford a fifteen-hundred-square-foot house with a pool in a great part of town. Police officers, Firemen, teachers, retail sales clerks...people with all sorts of jobs in Greenwich could not afford to live in Greenwich on their own. They commuted from nearby towns or shared housing, or both. His house was off Old Church Road. At the end of a narrow, winding, shared driveway, his driveway continued further away from the other homes. It curled around a gorgeous home that some would call a mansion, a separate multi-car garage, past a pool and down to his house. The building looked a bit like the main home and a bit like a renovated garage. It used to be the guesthouse for the main house, and now it was *his* house.

His grandparents used to own the main house, and much of the property around it between Old Church Road and Hillside Road. The naming of Hillside Road honored nearby "Put's Hill," where Revolutionary War General Israel Putnam escaped from the British in 1779 and went on to warn the neighboring town of Stamford. A historic marker sat near the intersection of Old Church Road and East Putnam Avenue, also known as the Boston Post Road, or just the Post Road for short. That's why the name Putnam was so popular in Greenwich, including the Putnam Bank & Trust. That famous hill was an L-shaped piece of land, part of it ran along the Post Road, and part of it ran parallel to Old Church Road. The main home of the Rollins property sat on top of the opposite end of that ridge from the historic marker.

The "new" Greenwich High School down a hill, through some woods and across a field from his house opened in the fall of 1970. About nine hundred students became the first graduating class in a brand-new facility in May of 1971. Three years earlier, Steven's ninth grade class at the Greenwich Country Day School had just eighty students. He did *not* go to Greenwich High, class of '71; instead, he attended a prep school about sixty miles away then went off to college and Hartford. Being relatively unknown in town had advantages, though. When people didn't know who he was, or care who he was, they would be more inclined to speak freely in his presence. He experienced this many times during his summer jobs growing up. Bankers and lawyers would discuss business deals while he carried their golf clubs at the Greenwich Country Club. Families and their friends would discuss everything under the sun, literally, just a few feet away from his lifeguard station at the club's pool. It wasn't eavesdropping, which is listening secretly to what is being said in private. A speaker's apathy creates a new category and removes guilt. Now, as a reporter in his hometown, he had a balance of connections and anonymity. Because he was tall, people

23

sometimes looked at him like they thought they knew him, or thought they *should* know him, but they couldn't figure it out. He was used to it, and those factors contributed to his personality and reporting skills. They actually became ones he relied upon.

On a Saturday morning in late March, he woke up, put a Beatles record on the Pioneer turntable, and lowered the needle. He heard the brief trumpet fanfare and the familiar opening line. "Roll up, roll up for the Mystery Tour, step right this way." The Beatles had been very popular in his household growing up. Since then his musical tastes had evolved a bit, as did all of the music in the 1970s, but he also enjoyed some old favorites. Coincidentally, "The Mystery Tour" was what some of his friends used to call their three-year stint at prep school. The song always reminded him of his first real girlfriend, Jessica Flagler.

They met when she was in tenth grade. She took a liking to him, and during a Saturday night school dance she gave him "The Look," an innocent-yet-not facial expression some girls used to wrap boys around their little fingers. He had not seen "The Look" before, and he fell for it: hook, line and sinker. He didn't mind being wrapped around her little finger, or her tight body, either, especially on the weekends, when they would sneak off to the adjacent golf course and find a quiet, secluded spot.

They dated for almost two years, but it turned out badly, very badly. Bad breakups at prep school were far worse than breakups at a local high school because parents felt more helpless being away from their sad or angry children, unable to hug and console them. Communication was far more one-sided and limited, which makes matters worse. That helplessness and a smoldering grudge were big problems because her father was a rich and powerful man. Albert D. Flagler was a direct descendant of John H. Flagler, a wealthy tycoon from the Civil War era, who not only founded an iron and steel company that merged with U.S. Steel, but also controlled the world's largest chain of drugstores. Coincidentally, the elder Flagler retired in Greenwich, but the family relocated to Boston after Albert's grandfather graduated from Harvard. Albert D. Flagler tried to have Steven suspended or even expelled, but then withdrew his effort because Jessica's tearful drama lacked substance and actually magnified her own blame and responsibility. It would have ruined her prep school career, too. The whole matter dissolved, but Steven would never forget when Mr. Flagler arrived at school to pick up his daughter for a weekend. Steven was with a group of friends standing outside the school's ivy-covered brick entrance near the Dean of Students' office. They were taking a break after classes and before they had to go to their sports practices. The group wasn't noisy, but emanated a murmur of teen excitement and laughter. It could have been any dozen students in the school, but with one exception—this group contained the tallest boy in school.

Mr. Flagler and Jessica were getting into their jet black 1969 Mercedes-Benz 300SEL 6.3 in the main circular driveway. Flagler noticed Steven while Jessica pretended to ignore him, looking vacantly in his general direction but not exactly at him. Mr. Flagler knew what he looked like because Steven had been to their estate occasionally in the summers. Steven was preoccupied with his group, leaving Flagler a head start in absorbing what was happening. Soon after, Steven looked at the cars parked in the main circle, and the man standing outside the magnificent German vehicle. It usually would have been a common sight, but not this time. The man's scowl was as serious as his suit. Steven was talking to his roommate when it dawned on him who he was looking at. The roommate stopped talking mid-sentence, looked at Steven, then across the circle at Flagler, then back at Steven before excusing himself and slipping back into the school building.

Flagler watched this minute unfold with a casual yet focused approach. Steven looked at him as his group drifted apart. Flagler pushed off the car's door and pivoted ninety degrees so he was facing squarely toward the front entrance. He stood with his heels slightly wider than shoulder width, slowly folded his arms across his chest, exhaled, and lowered his chin slightly, turning it a bit to the right. Flagler unleashed an ice-cold laser beam of a stare and didn't budge.

Steven was used to being confident and effective around school, in dorm rooms and classrooms. This situation didn't match any of those scenarios. It was probably a complete shock compared to what he was thinking about two minutes earlier. Flagler didn't move and didn't let up. Steven considered several options, but did nothing except squeeze the three-ring binder he was holding. He rocked forward in his Converse All-Stars like he was about to take a step forward then stopped. He started to speak then stopped. Flagler didn't move and didn't let up. Steven broke eye contact first. He looked down at his sneakers, then pushed the door and went back into the school. Flagler tracked him until he was completely out of sight before he budged one inch. He took a deep breath and reached to open the Mercedes. Steven made a promise to himself right then to be cautious about girls like Jessica, and their fathers.

It was a lesson from his prep school years he didn't like to remember but would never forget. He took the Beatles off the turntable, fished around a bit through his records on a bookshelf, and replaced it with Grand Funk Railroad's "We're an American Band."

Chapter Four

After his shower, Steven wandered back into the living room and flipped the stereo receiver's dial from LP to FM, turned it up, and left the front door open as he took *The New York Times* and a warm cup of Folgers coffee out to the pool. The water in the pool was still very cold, but the spring sunshine was warming the gray cement pool deck. He was wearing Levi's 501 jeans and his old gray University of Missouri hooded sweatshirt over a t-shirt. He counted on the sun and the coffee to warm him up as he read the newspaper and did its crossword puzzle. This was his frequent weekend ritual when the weather was nice enough. He usually read both *The New York Times* and the *Greenwich Time* every day. Like anyone in a particular field, he saw things in a slightly different way, like a pro athlete watching another game, or an actor watching a movie. He read the articles with the discerning, critical eye of an insider. He noted the styles of the authors and internally critiqued their sentence structures. It was ingrained in him, a trait that caught a spark at Greenwich Country Day, burned kindling at a prep school then turned into a full-blown blaze at college. He chose Missouri for its renowned Journalism program. There he could say he went to "Columbia" and people would smile knowingly. In Greenwich, he would catch himself and clarify the distinction so people wouldn't confuse it with the Ivy League school in New York City. Steven Rollins was not an Ivy Leaguer. He didn't try to be.

Steven took a sip of coffee, opened the newspaper to the crossword puzzle, and pushed up the sleeves of his sweatshirt. That Missouri J-School degree and some top-notch contacts helped him land his first job. His family was long-time friends with the family of Lowell Webster, who would become the town's Mayor when Steven was a teenager. Webster was a Congressman while Steven was in prep school, then a Senator while he was in college. Having a U.S. Senator's endorsement was like owning Willy Wonka's Golden Ticket. Steven cashed that in to get in the door with *The New York Times*, which was a staggering, monumental achievement for someone just out of college. *The Times* is by any definition one of the greatest newspapers in the world. It's where people aspire to finish their careers. Starting there was unheard of.

Steven was assigned to the newspaper's regional office in the state capitol of Hartford, which seemed like a good fit for the Connecticut native. He was fine when he focused on his writing, but the peripheral activities and demands were his undoing. After seven years of living in dorms and apartments, he was not interested in continuing that lifestyle near Hartford, not when he had a sweet bachelor pad in Greenwich, ninety minutes away. That commute made him less accessible to the whims of his editors, and it often took him out of the loop for social activities with other Hartford-based staffers, not that he had many invitations in the first place. He was the youngest writer there, by far. The older employees were jealous of their new silver-spoon kid and made things rough on him instead of taking him under their wings. The people closer to his age were far less educated, and worked in support positions, so he had no real peers there either. He thought he could focus on his assignments and block out everything else, but the challenge of doing "*Times* quality" work, the passive-aggressive working conditions and his commute were too much for a young man just out of school, even one with the talent and promise he had. It was a case of too much, too soon, and he knew it, so he figuratively barricaded himself into his home to search for a solution. Three pizzas, two six-packs, and one long weekend later, Steven had his next step figured out.

The senior editor of the *Hartford Courant* was more than pleased to find a resume of Steven's caliber on his desk. The *Hartford Courant* was the oldest continually published newspaper in the country. Even older than the United States, dating back to 1764, it was also the largest newspaper in the state. Steven started there and was given decent local stories. The more comfortable he became, the better he did. He quickly was given better assignments, and finished them quite well. That same commute to and from Greenwich didn't seem as bad, and he was treated at the *Courant* like a rising star.

The editor's faith in Steven turned out to be well founded. Steven excelled when he was given a chance to dig into political and state government coverage. The Watergate scandal dominated the headlines while he was in college.

Most people saw it as the demise of a President; however, Steven and many other journalism students were captivated and awestruck by the daily reporting angle— the idea that two reporters at *The Washington Post* could have such a profound impact on national events. To them Watergate wasn't about Richard Nixon and H.R. Haldeman, it was about Carl Bernstein and Bob Woodward, and they were living icons to a generation of writers. In their world, reporters were rock stars, typewriters were guitars, and breaking a big story was like having a Top 40 hit. That was his mindset with the *Courant*.

Steven was doing well covering state government. His stories were well received and he was making a name for himself. He maintained his connections from his stint at *The Times* and added to them with his initiative and dedication at the *Courant*. Republican Ella Grassley was the Governor at the time and she had close ties to fellow Republican, Senator Lowell Webster. Governor Grassley knew who Steven was, and after Senator Webster vouched for him during a casual conversation, Grassley invited Steven to her office in the Capitol Building. Steven had seen her at events and press conferences, but they had never spoken before. Their conversation went well. They talked about Senator Webster and his family, and it turned out she knew the headmaster at his prep school, thirty-five miles down the road in Watertown.

"Well, Steven, you have quite a background."

"Thank you, Governor."

"You've been in Hartford with *The Times* also?"

"Yes, that's right."

"I thought I recognized you from some press conferences here."

"I must have been standing up if you did."

Grassley laughed. "I'll tell you what. Tomorrow afternoon I am making an announcement about energy."

"Yes, I saw that on your schedule."

"Well, here's what it's about. It's right after a meeting with the president of General Electric. They want to do a test project right here, and modernize a power plant on the Connecticut River. If their research is accurate, it will create substantial savings for thousands of customers here."

"That sounds pretty impressive."

"It certainly is. Here's the phone number for his press liaison. Wait an hour or so before you call him, and he will already know your name and that you're writing a preview article." She pushed a business card across her gleaming mahogany desk.

"Thank you, Governor, I appreciate it."

"It's been a pleasure meeting you. I'll see you tomorrow."

"Yes, thanks again."

The huge exclusive splashed across the front page the next day. At the energy event, the Governor made eye contact with him and nodded slightly. Needless to say, the reporter from the Hartford office of *The Times* was not as happy. Steven Rollins was rolling.

A few months later, Steven caught wind that a media conglomerate was about to buy the *Courant*. He cringed when he found out the company's CEO was none other than Albert D. Flagler. Yes, Jessica's father. Flagler lived in Boston but had powerful friends in both states. He occasionally lit up Hartford's black tie social scene. More importantly, Steven dreaded having Flagler in the *Courant's* hierarchy. Steven doubted he could fly under the radar without Flagler noticing him, not when his name is in the newspaper almost daily. He was also pretty certain Flagler would remember their prep school fiasco and hold it against him, *but to what degree*? It could be anywhere from merely downgrading his assignments to squelching raises and promotions to an outright death sentence, and he feared the latter was more likely. Steven was really upset by this development. He was really starting to feel accepted and successful writing at the *Courant* and had even made a few good friends on the staff. To them, it was more important that he was a Connecticut native than having a degree from Missouri J-school. He went to talk to Bill Bowman, the man who hired him.

"Hey Boss, got a minute?"

"Sure, what's up?"

Steven closed the door to block out the din of the busy newsroom.

"Well, I've heard rumblings that a group from Boston is about to buy our paper."

"I'm surprised the rumor leaked out, but I'm not surprised *you're* the one who found out. I don't know much; that's going on in the big offices upstairs, you know?"

"Yes, but I have a problem."

"What is it?"

"I know the CEO of that group but not in a good way, a man named Flagler."

"What do you mean?"

"I'm pretty sure he holds a long-standing grudge against me. It's personal…it involves his family."

"Oh," Bowman said, as he slumped back into his chair.

"Yeah, like I said, it's personal, and pretty toxic. I'm really nervous about it."

"That's horrible. Officially, I can't say anything. Unofficially, I know you're a smart guy, so do what you gotta do, and let me know if I can help."

"Thanks, Boss."

"Be careful, and good luck."

Steven left the meeting feeling dejected, but in the time it took him to walk back to his desk, he built up an inner fire to fight, so he did what any good reporter would do…he worked his connections on the phone to learn more.

Being a graduate of the University of Missouri's School of Journalism was a blessing. His fellow alums were like a fiercely loyal fraternity. He left the campus with his diploma and a U.M. Alumni Guidebook. He felt comfortable calling anyone in it because just mentioning Missouri J-School opened doors. He looked under the cross-reference for Massachusetts, and found several names in the Boston area. One worked for *The Boston Globe*, and two worked in Public Relations and Media Relations for a company affiliated with Flagler's business. One of the men was a senior when Steven was a freshman, and Steven hoped he would remember him from intramural basketball and some parties. He was right. The VP of Media Relations remembered him, and said he was happy to help. Steven explained his call was not to break the story of the acquisition, not yet, anyway. At this point he was more interested in pending firings and consolidations, in particular, his own job security. The VP promised to look around to see what he could find out.

For two days Steven was beyond distracted and dazed. People asked him what was wrong, but he couldn't begin to explain it. He didn't eat or sleep much. He felt like he did when Flagler was pursuing his prep school expulsion. Then the phone call came in from his alumni-friend in Boston. The VP was able to see, but not copy or take, the list of expected cuts on the *Courant* staff. The names included staff in duplicate areas or very narrow specialty fields, and others that were high pay but low production, that is, people who could be easily replaced by someone half their age at half their salary. Steven was far from high salary and low output. He was starting to feel relieved until he heard the word "but." The VP said his name was on the list, the only one hand-written and marked in a yellow highlighter, in fact. The initials "A.D.F." were written next to his name and circled. Flagler had remembered him, and personally signed off on adding him to the layoffs. The VP apologized and tried to say something nice to cheer him up. Steven didn't hear half of it, but thanked the VP for his hard work, which was very helpful even though it wasn't the outcome he wanted to hear.

The next day he met with Bowman again.

"Hey, Boss."

"Hi," Bowman said, motioning to the seat. Steven closed the door.

"I looked into the Boston group's takeover, and I got some inside information."

"Really? That was quick."

"My contact in their office saw some paperwork. They've already decided who they're gonna fire when the deal goes through. There's a list."

"Oh my." Bowman was genuinely astonished.

"Yeah, it's a full page, and, well… my name is on that list." Steven could barely get that sentence out of his mouth.

"Oh no. Any chance that's a mistake?" Bowman asked.

"I don't think so. It's in alphabetical order or I'd be on top. My contact saw the list. As an extra favor he skimmed for your name, but you're safe."

"Thank you. So who's out?"

"Mostly older reporters and duplicate beats. I'm neither, so I know Flagler still has it in for me. I can't be here when that goes down. I *know* I'll be fired."

"Steven, you're one of my best reporters. I can't afford to lose you."

"Thanks… but I'm walking in the gallows. I can't let that happen to me."

"But I'll go to bat for you."

"I appreciate that, I really do, but Flagler, you can't bat against that. He's got a Nolan Ryan fastball. You've been nothing but great to me, and I love it here, but I gotta go while I can. I'm sad to say, very sad…I have to resign."

"Are you sure?"

"Yeah," Steven sighed. "I'm sorry, Boss."

"Me too."

For the second time in a couple of years, Steven was out. Like in the Beatles song, "The fool on the hill sees the sun going down." He gave his notice, claimed "personal reasons," and headed back to his hometown. His last drive was the longest ever, thanks to the remnants of one of the worst blizzards in New England's history. The February 1978 storm set snowfall records in several cities. Governor Grassley had ordered all the state's roads closed except for emergency travel for three days. When that ban was lifted, he headed home, feeling like he had survived a storm of his own as he navigated through the snow banks that loomed on both sides of the Merritt Parkway. That afternoon the ninety miles felt like nine hundred. He turned on the radio, found WTIC, and the next song was Foreigner's "Long, Long Way from Home."

Steven loved Greenwich, a town of fifty square miles and about sixty thousand people. He knew with his degree and connections he could get a job with the local newspaper at the drop of a hat, despite his recently spotty background. He also knew there was nowhere else to go if he blew it.

At the *Greenwich Time*, he immediately broke the news that media conglomerate's intended purchase of the *Courant*. The *Courant* was a day behind, which pleased his new bosses in Greenwich. He was back on his game. He was sure the *Time* was off Albert D. Flagler's radar, especially while he was busy with this major piece of business. Flagler read *The Wall Street Journal* and *The Boston Globe*, not local newspapers.

Coming home was a chance for a fresh start, take a personal inventory, and start the long and winding road back to the upper levels of his chosen career. For several months he was doing just that and was happy about it, but he couldn't rest after that big story or some of his other recent work, most notably, a scandal involving the Bruce Park Tavern. He made a promise to himself to be committed to doing what was necessary to re-launch his life, his career, and to reclaim the "s" he lost, going from *The Times* to the *Time*.

Still outside by the pool, Steven folded his newspaper and lifted his empty coffee cup. He walked back inside to make a phone call.

Chapter Five

"Boys, it's Bingo Night, and I'm not talking about the geezers down at the Rec. Center. B-nine, bingo, See ya!" Mark said.

"Yeah, later, Mark."

Mark smiled as his two friends slapped open the main doors at the YMCA entrance and hopped down the wide granite stairs. Friday evenings were usually slow at the Y, with people taking the night off from their workouts to get a head start on the weekend. There was a steady stream of phone calls and walk-ins though, not for info about swimming lessons, but for info on the weekend party plans. For Mark's friends and others, the "Four Aces" held all the cards. They all knew the scoop, and worked in places that had decent traffic for people, info, and occasionally some illicit activity. For those who couldn't retrieve a phone message at home or work, this was the next best choice, perhaps even better. The "Aces" were Mark at the Y, Frank Castino, the owner and primary bartender at Bruce Park Tavern, Alex Henderson at the Bowling Lanes, and "Backcountry Bobby" Landry at The Old Country House in Banksville. Mark went to

Greenwich High with Frank and Alex, and his family had known Bobby's since before either of them was born. Bobby was a year ahead of them in school, but they still hung out together.

Back in those school days, when they were old enough to drive but not old enough to legally be in clubs (which deterred them only slightly), they took turns hosting Saturday night poker games in their parents' basements. These parties had a tendency to become quite raucous, especially when the parents were not home, which often determined where the card game/party would be held. That's how they became known as the "Four Aces," a moniker each of them took seriously, and took pride in adopting. People would come not for the cards, but for the party going on around the game. More often than not the games were at Frank's house. His father owned and ran Bruce Park Tavern back then and usually worked on Saturday nights. Frank's mother liked to go out on Saturday nights with her friends or help Frank's father at the Tavern. The Castinos' finished basement looked like a bar and was stocked like one, too. It had a Las Vegas-style card table, a pool table, a dartboard, a TV and a big stereo. Some of their friends called it "The Castino Casino." It elevated Frank's status to the Ace of Spades.

Even after the Saturday night cards games faded away, these four remained influential in coordinating party plans. Now they were all still single and in visible management jobs, but right then they were more interested in managing the weekend... especially *that* weekend, the start of Spring Break, the traditional kickoff to the party season, when the weather, women and whiskey all seem to get better. There were plenty of single people around their ages who lived in town, or at least it seemed like it. Plus, the college kids were back home for the week, so the nightlife kicked up a notch in both atmosphere and *some* potential...excluding of course the younger college girls trying too hard with the Bonnie Bell Lip Smackers and Lee Press On Nails.

Bingo? B-9? It was a code, a plan, a progression. Five places, all starting with B-I-N-G-O, an hour or so at each starting at nine o'clock. It's not like they convoyed around like C.W. McCall when the big hand hit twelve, but it was an outline of their intent. People made their plans around it, adding and subtracting locations, substituting here and there. Those who wanted to hang out with most of the core crew played Bingo for at least part of the night.

Mark cleaned up, put on a fresh rugby shirt, closed the Y, and headed out to start the game. "B-9" meant Bruce Park Tavern, nine o'clock. When Mark walked in, Frank smiled at him and cocked his head to the left. Yes, their usual long table in the back left corner was filling up. As usual, it was semi-reserved for them on Friday nights. Mark slid into a bench seat where five friends were already ripping and roaring. He grabbed the pitcher of beer and surveyed the array of homemade pizza.

"What's up, Mark?" one friend said.

"Hey, how's it going?" another asked.

"Cool, man, cool. What we got here?" Mark asked.

"All of it. Bacon and onion, meatball and mushroom, sausage and pep. It's all good!"

"Bud?"

"Of course."

"Dig it!"

The hot slice of pizza singed the roof of Mark's mouth for a moment before the cold beer soothed the sting. Bruce Park Tavern was a great launching spot for the guys. They would catch up on the news of the week, do some dreaming and scheming, play some tabletop shuffleboard and shoot the breeze, spraying around salty language without worrying about who might be offended. Pitchers of beer on the house didn't hurt, either.

The shuffleboard was the Tavern's unique feature and was quite popular. It was similar to the more common outdoor version but on a reduced scale. The wood playing surface was as long as two pool tables end-to-end, but only about two feet wide, and raised about three feet off the floor. The board ran along the right wall of the Tavern, parallel to the bar on the left, which created a funneling effect back to the tables, kitchen, and bathrooms. There were big tournaments every three months or so, and casual play virtually every day. Those casual games often involved wagering, but with house-mandated limits to avoid fights. There was a winner and a loser, which was fine, with the usual stakes of the loser buying the winner a beer, or a pitcher. The only shuffleboard table in town was a big draw at the Tavern.

A closer look revealed table shuffleboard had stages of each turn that could be broken down into specific components. A player would have to determine a strategy then physically attempt to execute a shot to match the path he visualized for the puck. This middle portion of the shot, like in golf, basketball and other sports, was a suspended-in-time moment of waiting for the results. After that second or so of anticipation, there was a payoff. Did the puck land in a scoring area? Did it knock an opponent out of a scoring area, or worse yet, knock one of his own pucks out of one? If it missed, did it create interference (good or bad), or fly off the board entirely? Fractions of inches could have wide-ranging results. Finally, the aftermath: possibly an emotional reaction, points and position gained and lost, and then yielding to the other player's analysis of a fresh situation, as the process renewed. An entire micro-life cycle existed in the simple slide of a metal and plastic puck across a long wooden board to a target area. Perhaps at a primal level, that's what made the game so appealing, and a fixture at the Tavern. This night was no different, with four men beginning to play doubles and deciding on the order in which they would proceed to start a new game.

Meeting at the Tavern was also a chance to talk to Frank face-to-face. Frank looked beat down and tired, more than usual. Even though he was their friend, his expression indicated he wasn't in the mood to talk more than the expected bartender banter. Mark wasn't surprised; he knew Frank needed a big summer to make up for a really bad winter. He had been struggling since his father's fatal heart attack on Thanksgiving night. Frank had been enjoying working alongside his father, learning the ropes until Senior decided to work part-time and eventually retire. Now Frank was thrust into inheriting and running the Tavern right away. He was also forced to deal with the grief of his father's death in a workplace that seemed to reflect his father's image in every polished section of the bar, in every clean glass mug, and in the eyes of every regular customer.

Mark's Timex watch, made popular by John Cameron Swayze, showed 10:10 when he left. The Bingo's "I-10" was the Indian Harbor Inn, with a big deck and outdoor bar overlooking Long Island Sound. This place could be hit or miss since it was at a marina. Some nights it was overrun by preppies in Top-Siders, corduroys, and Lacoste shirts, glowing in the reflected wealth of Daddy's yacht. There might be groups of housewives enjoying an evening out, or brokers huddled together, unable to leave their Wall Street chatter on the train. In the summer when the evenings were warm, this place really hopped, but it was too chilly that night for the deck to be lively. Still, it was worth a look.

Bingo's "N-11" was Nero's on the Post Road near the top of Greenwich Avenue, the heart of the town's retail area. The locals called it simply "the Avenue," in much the same way Greenwich High School was "the High School" and New York was "the City." Filled with brass, ferns, and mirrors, Nero's was definitely the most upscale of the spots on the card. It was very popular with people older than Mark, in their thirties and forties, looking for a respectable but fun night out. Those folks usually emptied out by 11:45 so they could be home to pay their babysitters by midnight. They were probably already somewhat dreading waking up early Saturday for their kids' sports games or ballet classes. Maybe they didn't feel it was appropriate for people their age to be out past midnight or maybe their babysitter had a curfew. Mark still identified with those who believed the best part of the night often *started* at midnight. A Nero's stop also meant a swing across the street to the Bowling Lanes. A big bar and restaurant, thirty-six lanes, plus a large, well-lit parking lot in central Greenwich made for an attractive combination. Even if you didn't like bowling, you could pick up some strikes and spares at the Lanes.

Alex was the Assistant Manager at the Lanes by title and also the unofficial Social Director in reality. He had worked at the Lanes since high school when he sprayed and sorted shoes and passed out scoring sheets and pencils. The series of managers he worked for all had one thing in common—they recognized his rare ability to bring customers, particularly attractive female customers, into the Lanes, and not just mothers and *au pairs* shepherding groups of nine-year-olds. Alex could have passed for Robert Redford's younger brother with his blonde hair and piercing blue eyes, but he also had Opie Taylor's naïveté, so he didn't fully capitalize on his dazzling potential. That made him even more appealing to the women whose shopping outings downtown now included meeting their friends for drinks, lunch or actual bowling at the Lanes. A manager recognized this social phenomenon as a marketing opportunity and gave it his full endorsement by creating a Ladies' Night. It was popular and successful on its own, and did even better once the single men in town realized so many single and not-so-single women were congregating in a place they liked going to anyway. At its peak, Ladies' Night at the Lanes outdrew similar promotions at just about every other bar or club in town, all because the sweet and somewhat oblivious young man with movie star good looks and a humble disposition was at the center of it. Alex was the Ace of Hearts of the "Four Aces."

Three guys from Bruce Park Tavern and about eight new people were already at Nero's. Mark spotted them, held up one finger and waggled it toward the busy bar. On Mark's way to ordering a drink he passed a table where none other than Patty Callahan was talking with three people. She saw him, but she was too involved in listening to her friends to break out of their conversation. Plus, it wasn't clear what was going on since that ten-spot fluttered out of the Y's ceiling tiles a month ago. Mark leaned onto the bar, waited for the bartender, and looked over again to see who was with his group.

At the same time, Patty took an inconspicuous glance at Mark as she brushed her hair off her left shoulder then turned back to her conversation. One friend was an accountant, David Olson. He was talking about how busy he had been over the past four weeks doing tax returns. More than half of his annual business was done in March and April. In addition to David's deadline and workload pressures, many of his wealthy clients had complex accounts and portfolios, finely tuned to maximize their fortunes. Tonight was his first weeknight out in close to two months, so he loosened his tie, literally and figuratively. The friend to his right, across the table from Patty, worked for the town in the Parks & Recreation Department. Ronny Graham was talking about how he was just *entering* his busy season, not finishing it. From just before Easter up to Memorial Day, his in-box was full with applications and payments for annual beach passes, marina slip renewals, summer camp registrations, a spring road running race, and a seemingly endless amount of baseball and softball teams playing in leagues and tournaments. That included the Memorial Day Weekend Softball Celebration, which was held at several parks at the same time. Ronny said the financial crush dropped off but stayed somewhat steady through the summer, then peaked again for the Labor Day Weekend Festival, which included pony rides, carnival games and activities on the High School's playing fields, and a big concert that filled the football stadium.

Ronny had been a star athlete at the High School. He was a starter in three sports, making All-State in one and All-County in another. He had a passion and a flair for working with children. He ran the town's summer Little League program while he was still in college. During a baseball practice a few summers earlier, he wrecked his knee when he stepped on a sprinkler head as he chased a fly ball. That injury led to his decision to major in Sports Administration and make that his career. His reputation and credentials were enough to get him a position in town.

His family name, in particular being Police Chief Ray Graham's younger brother, made him even easier to hire. Ronny told Patty and the others he liked the sports side of the job, but didn't like the overload of financial filings and paperwork. The town made a significant percentage of its annual one hundred million dollar budget through Parks & Rec. It brought in nearly five hundred thousand dollars on beach passes alone. Patty listened closely as Ronny briefly outlined the department's budget.

The third friend was sitting to Patty's left. Ronny's longtime girlfriend Jennifer Johnstone worked for a travel agency and had been very busy too. Over the last several weeks she had been booking Easter vacations for Greenwich's upper-crust: ski trips to Aspen, Killington, and Lake Placid, site of the upcoming 1980 Winter Olympics. She arranged beach trips to Hobe Sound, Jupiter, and Bermuda, cruises out of Miami and excursions to Europe, too. Jennifer sighed about all these great places she knew only through brochures and her clients' stories. Patty knew how she felt.

"What about the Bahamas?" Patty asked. "I've been a few times on vacation and I've always dreamed of living there." Patty and Jennifer talked about Nassau and Paradise Island. Patty made a promise to herself to visit the Bahamas again, especially now that she was old enough to really enjoy it.

At the end of their night, the friends shared hugs and said goodnight. Jennifer didn't notice, but Patty hugged Ronny about three seconds longer and slightly tighter than she normally would have. Ronny didn't mind, but didn't show any reaction.

"G-12" on Bingo Night was flexible. It either meant Garbo's, a flashy disco a few miles farther down the Post Road, or The Greek's, a diner across town. Those were two vastly different choices: more drinks, dancing and debauchery, or shoveling down some late night food. It also required some planning ahead because of the stricter dress code at the glitzy Garbo's.

"O-1" for Mark was non-negotiable. The Old Country House in Banksville was his home turf, just a mile or so from his house. He could walk home or get a ride if he had to, and had done so several times after having "a drink" turned into a bottle. His buddy Backcountry Bobby had Mark's name pretty much typed into the nightly pass list. He never had to wait in line on the gravel parking lot in front of the low-slung, wood building. Being just across the state line, The Old Country House was open later than the bars in Connecticut, which made North Street a target-rich territory for Greenwich Police looking for drunk drivers coming back to town. Mark sometimes called Bobby "Clubby," which combined his standing at The Old Country House and his Ace of Clubs status with the "Four Aces." Bobby seemed to know most of the people there that night, and kept up with the gossip about his peers who lived north of the Merritt Parkway, in the "backcountry." Bobby told Mark several times, "Hang around some liquored-up people who are still coherent, and it is amazing what they will say and what you can learn."

Mark swore his Camaro had some sort of built-in autopilot. He made it home safely, and the black Panasonic

clock radio next to his bed flipped a digit and read three-something. Next thing he knew he looked again and it was 11:24, with the sun shining through the window. He jumped out of bed as his adrenaline kicked in, threw on a Yankees shirt, jeans, and adidas Superstars. He sloshed a cup of coffee from the banged-up metal pot in the kitchen, called out a goodbye to his mother in the living room, and drove that Camaro down to Central Junior High School.

Chapter Six

The fly ball was a white speck against the bright blue sky. It grew larger and larger until it settled into a well-worn Rawlings glove. Steven smiled and flipped one of the team's ten practice balls back toward the dusty infield. It had been a sunny and dry week in the middle of April, so a few guys from the YMCA team were finally able to break out their softball gear and clear out some of the winter cobwebs before the season started. He was pleased to step away from his typewriter and notebooks and enjoy the fresh air, sunshine, sports and conversation. He was looking forward to his second season with the team. He was friendly with the guys but not really friends. Actually, he rarely saw any of them outside of these games. There were two cores of the team...Mark's high school buddies and people from the YMCA. The key was Mark knew everybody. Everyone was about the same age and there was some overlap between the groups, but there was no reason for any friction. Most of them were there to get out of the house, be social, channel their competitive urges, and perhaps sweat out some of the alcohol in their systems from the night before. Steven was pretty sure that Mark's sunglasses had as much to do with the night before as they did with the clear sky that afternoon. He decided to needle him about it.

"Hey Mark, what's with the shades?"

"It's sunny out here, man," Mark said.

"They're really helping you field those grounders."

"Shut up, you big giraffe. Why don't you go play some basketball or something?"

"Whoa," a few of the guys chimed in, in a chorus of amusement.

"Good one, midget. Why don't you go play *miniature* golf?" Steven responded.

"Whoa!" the guys howled, as practice came to a halt.

Steven started dancing like a Muhammad Ali throwing punches. "Float like a butterfly, sting like a bee!" he said.

Mark grunted. Steven threw another verbal haymaker.

"Hey, nice shirt, Mister Bandwagon," Steven said, referring to the 1978 World Champion Yankees.

"Whoooa!" the chorus rang.

"Bull. That's my team. My Dad loved DiMaggio and Mantle," Mark said.

53

"Yeah, and the Pittsburgh Steelers and UCLA basketball too, I bet."

"Shut up, man. I'm too hung over for this," Mark said.

"I knew it!" Steven shouted.

"Whoop-de-do, Mister Reporter. Big scoop there, front page for the *Daily Planet*," Mark hollered.

Everyone got a big laugh out of that, even Steven. He went over and gave Mark a playful hug across his shoulders. Mark pushed back. "You're a big goofball, man," he said, laughing.

The team came together from all parts of town, with different jobs and backgrounds. The players had all attended public schools, except for Steven and the third baseman, Chris Daniel, who graduated from St. Mary's, the town's Catholic high school. Chris was one of Steven's longest-lasting friends. They were in the same homeroom in fourth and sixth grades, and were baseball teammates and classmates through ninth grade at Greenwich Country Day. They played on the same Babe Ruth League team during two of their high school summers. Chris was the one friend from Steven's childhood that he still kept in touch with on a regular basis, with baseball, and now softball, being the cornerstone of their friendship.

The guys knew Steven worked for the newspaper, but it usually did not matter much to them, unless something in the paper struck too close to home. They weren't very interested in the latest news from the Planning and Zoning Commission or budget hearings. Besides, when they were together playing ball, nothing else mattered, and they either temporarily forgot or didn't care that Steven was a reporter. It was an unspoken bond that everything said there was off the record, and he never abused that trust. However, with reporting in his blood and possessing a sharp memory and affinity for details, he soaked it all in, even if most of it filtered out shortly thereafter. He was rarely completely off the clock.

When Steven was working, he usually started his days with the morning briefing at the Police Department, just off the Avenue. Sergeant Bill Sanderson would address the reporters and pass around a redacted sheet listing the latest arrests, charges, details, and court dates. Sometimes a reporter would ask if Chief Graham would come out to provide a quote about an arrest. Much of that information was classified, but occasionally Steven would raise an eyebrow when he recognized a name, usually for something like a speeding ticket or a DWI. That's what happened a few months earlier when a case came up involving Frank Castino, one of Mark's close friends. An off-duty cop was at Bruce Park Tavern having a beer when some underage drinking got out of hand, which in itself was not a big deal or all that unusual. The problem was one of the underage girls was the Fire Chief's daughter, and she had a marijuana pipe in her pocket that she said belonged to "a friend." Well, that caused a political firestorm all across town government, and the watchdog groups wanted to ensure the girl was not receiving any preferential treatment.

That would be enough to keep the gossip flowing in any small town, but then the follow-up investigation found more dirt. The story escalated into a multi-layer mess so engrossing it became known simply as "The Scandal." The State Department of Alcohol, Tobacco and Firearms frowned at the unlicensed sawed-off shotgun that was kept behind the bar. That frown turned into a full-fledged scowl when agents found a locker in the back room filled with handguns, rifles, ammunition, and other weapons.

Two of Frank's managers took the rap for that. They were arrested for trafficking weapons and selling surplus alcohol out the back door. They were quickly convicted and sent to State Prison in Bridgeport. The surplus alcohol sales caught the attention of the State Department of Revenue. Their investigation found, among other things, the Tavern's business taxes were several years in arrears, dating back to when Frank took over for his father. Frank swore a blue streak at his accountant before, during, and after firing him. He sold his boat, gave up his highly coveted slip in the marina, and gouged a deep chunk out of his savings to pay the overdue taxes and the fines from both agencies. His liquor license was suspended for ninety days and the Tavern was closed for thirty days as part of a plea bargain for having several serious charges converted to suspended sentences with probation. Many observers thought he was lucky to get off with that penalty and most people forgot about the Fire Chief's daughter.

All the while, Steven used his state capital connections in Hartford to stay spot-on with his reporting of "The Scandal," earning him praise from the newspaper's publisher and a major regional award, their first in three years. However, he earned the scorn and contempt of Frank and his close friends, who saw Steven as a scapegoat for the trouble Frank was in. He was *persona non grata* at the Tavern, to put it mildly. Steven received a barrage of anonymous threats, including messages and mail threatening to "kick his butt" and even worse. His car's tires were slashed and the hood was keyed with a deep, nasty gorge making an X. After he spotted headlights circling in and out of his driveway late at night, he applied for and received a restraining order against Frank to force him to keep his distance. He also changed to an unlisted phone number and developed a degree of paranoia about his personal safety in public.

During softball practice, a few of the guys were talking about the Tavern, which sponsored a team in their league, a pretty strong team actually.

"So, who's in the league this year?"

"Richard's, D'Elia Honda, Murphy's, Byram Builders, Food Mart, the usuals…and the Tavern's back, too."

"Frankie's puttin' up a team? I thought this year he'd drop out for sure."

"No way, he loves softball and baseball, and his teams bring people through the door, especially in the daytime."

"I heard he sold his boat because he couldn't afford it. I figured sponsoring teams was out, too."

"Yeah, the Tavern's been dead lately. I heard…"

"Hey, shhh."

Steven couldn't tell at first if the guys were talking about the Tavern's softball team, recounting tales from the night before or "The Scandal." He noticed they quieted down when he left Chris and approached them, which gave him his answer. To some of Mark's friends, he had messed with one of the "Four Aces," the Ace of Spades, actually, even though it was Steven's job and Chief Graham's investigation.

Steven had developed a strong relationship with Chief Graham. Ray Graham had been a Vietnam War hero, winner of a Silver Star, Purple Heart, and all sorts of tributes. His return home was a media spectacle, covered by all the New York City newspapers, the network TV news, and a cover story in *Life*. There was a huge parade for him in Greenwich right down the Avenue. It seemed the confetti was still being swept up when Graham was made Chief of Police, a position that opened up when the town accelerated the former Chief's retirement with a lucrative buy-out. Town leaders figured it was worth the publicity to have a great war-hero in a prominent position. They also correctly predicted the department would rally around Graham and buoy him until he became comfortable with the nuances of his job. Steven wrote a glowing feature story on Chief Graham for an anniversary of his homecoming, and they continued to get along quite well.

After softball practice, Steven grabbed his bat, the same Bombat he bought at the Greenwich Sport Shop the year before. He had been buying baseball cards and assorted equipment there since he was a kid. The bat was special-ordered from the factory in North Carolina, and Steven was pretty sure it was the only one in town. He slid into the front bench seat of the pale yellow 1970 Oldsmobile Cutlass that used to be his grandfather's. It had close to one hundred thousand miles on it, was paid off, and ran great. Those last two points were music to his ears. Not having a car payment or the hassle of frequent repairs was quite liberating. As he headed to White's Diner, he dug through a cassette storage crate that doubled as an armrest and chose a Bruce Springsteen tape with the tabs snapped off but taped over. A couple of the New York City radio stations caught on to the New Jersey singer early, before he was on the magazine covers of *Time* and *Newsweek* simultaneously in 1975. Steven went to one of his concerts at Madison Square Garden the previous summer. He still loved the Beatles and the music of his teenage years, but Springsteen was high on his list of current music he liked. He listened to "Thunder Road" on Stanwich Road and the Post Road to the Diner.

His usual seat in the booth by the window was open. As he had also hoped, Susie was working. She scooted right over with a menu and silverware.

"How ya doin', Mr. Rollins?" Susie said, playfully.

"Pretty good, Miss Baker, thanks. Just played some softball and grabbing some lunch before I head home," he

59

explained, even though Susie was used to having customers in sweats and sports clothes.

"How about a cheeseburger, fries, Cole slaw, and a large ice water?" he asked without looking at the menu.

"Okay, I'll have it in a minute," Susie said. She smiled again and walked quickly to the kitchen. She dictated the order through the window then wrote it down on the raised stainless steel shelf in front of the kitchen. She was standing in profile to Steven. He had a perfect angle to see her, between two stools and an empty table. He liked what he saw.

Susie was 5' 8" or 5' 9", with long legs and a medium build. Working on her feet was probably part of the reason she was in good shape. If she exercised, it wasn't at the Y, as far as he knew. The gene pool did her favors, because even with her hair up and wearing a uniform and an apron, she had a certain look about her. She had a pretty face but it showed a trace of crow's feet around her green eyes. Based on their previous conversations he thought she was about thirty years old, but looked younger, except for those crow's feet. She had worries beyond what most thirty-year-olds should, but no one ever knew due to her easy-going nature. They had developed a good rapport in the Diner, but Steven wanted to see how that would translate in a different, more private setting.

After finishing his lunch, he paid his bill, rounding way up to leave a generous tip. "So Susie," he said, "nothing against your top-notch crew in the kitchen, but how 'bout we raise the level of the dining experience some night and I take you out to dinner?"

Susie paused and looked like she was doing some quick calculations in her head as she scratched her right eyebrow. She lowered her hand, revealing a sincere smile on her face. "Yes, I'd like that," she said.

Susie slipped him her phone number. She watched him leave the Diner, closed her eyes for a second then went back to the kitchen.

A few days later in a small town north of Greenwich, Postal employees were sorting mail. Some letters were being put in bins to go out to local addresses, and the rest were placed in a different hopper to stay inside for the walk-up mailboxes housed in that building. One employee was taking smaller batches of that mail and popping letters into the appropriate boxes. He knew most of them by heart, matching the name and number with the box's location on the huge wall. He did a double take when he read the next envelope. It was an unfamiliar name, so he went behind the desk and compared it to the master list of mailboxes. It was a new entry, so he made a note to himself, went back to the wall, and slid the letter into Box 222, addressed to Greenwich Parking, Reconstruction and Resurfacing.

Chapter Seven

"C'mon kid, you got this guy. Let's go, let's go!"

Steven smoothed out the dirt around first base and shouted more encouragement to the pitcher. It was the YMCA softball team's first of two league games before the Memorial Day Weekend Softball Celebration tournament. He was taking his position when he heard two car doors slam and saw a flash of yellow and red in his peripheral vision to his left. He looked over between pitches and saw two attractive young women he didn't know. Patty and Jennifer walked toward the bleachers behind the team's bench on the first base side. Their brightly colored shirts were what caught his eye. Steven wasn't alone in making this observation. The game paused briefly as other players noticed the new spectators. Even Mark in left field unfolded his arms and took a more athletic stance. Girls like Patty and Jennifer could make an entrance simply by showing up, whether their nonchalance was intentional or not, especially in front of twenty to thirty guys who were mostly twenty to thirty years old. Some of the guys may have had fleeting and wishful thoughts of "green light," despite the girls' yellow and red shirts, which signified to Steven "caution" and "stop." The girls sat together at the end of the third row of the nearly empty bleachers, coincidentally crossed their legs in the same direction, and watched the game.

Jennifer lived with her parents less than a mile away. Her father was absent most of the time, traveling internationally on business. That's how she became interested in the travel industry. Jennifer couldn't go on her father's exotic trips, and even now she didn't travel as much as she would have liked to. Her trips seemed ordinary, not exotic, unless they were bolstered by her Dad's airline deals. Patty and Jennifer chatted about travel, work, and men, but nothing significant about any of the men they were watching, except for one. It was May, and they were mentally still used to anticipating summer vacations with fun and freedom, but now they had full-time jobs and were stuck working indoors. It was a much bigger adjustment than not having a two-week Christmas vacation or a week off for Spring Break. Jennifer seemed resigned to it, but Patty didn't like it at all. In fact, she truly hated the idea.

The girls had come from lunch on Sound Beach Avenue, just around the corner in the opposite direction. They were there to watch the game — Patty knew several of the guys on the YMCA team — and also to find out if there were any interesting outings planned for that night. Mark and his friends would certainly know that. They were also there because Jennifer expected to see Ronny for a few minutes. An inning or so later Ronny walked up, wearing blue jeans and his white Greenwich Parks & Recreation Department golf shirt. He was working on a Saturday afternoon, but was happy to be outdoors instead of inside his office. He was making the rounds, which included the ball fields at Binney Park. He timed his arrival with the YMCA's game.

Jennifer jumped up from the bleachers and hurried the thirty feet to meet him. She stood on her toes to give him a kiss and they talked for a minute. They continued talking as they headed back to the worn, wooden bleachers. Jennifer took her seat again as Ronny's attention shifted to the players and the umpires. He wanted to make sure everything was going well on the league's Opening Day. Umpire Zeke Belton and a few of the players waved and called out to Ronny. To former classmates at the High School and to many others, Ronny was one of the town's most recognizable athletes of his era, up to the versatile left-handed quarterback who tore up the Fairfield County league the previous fall. Ronny still moved with the grace and confidence of an athlete. He was happy to be recognized, but it didn't match the adulation of his high school days. He didn't talk about it, but he often wondered if his best days were behind him already. He was All-State before; now he wasn't even the most popular or famous member of his own family. That title went to his big brother, national celebrity/war-hero/Police Chief Ray Graham. Ronny was still struggling mightily with the transition out of the spotlight, and he told himself better days were coming.

While the teams were switching sides at the end of an inning, Patty piped up and said, "Hey, can I talk to you about the Swim Camp idea?"

"Sure, come walk with me so I can see two fields at once," Ronny replied. "Just a few minutes," he said to Jennifer. They walked down one of the foul lines until he came to a stop.

"The Swim Camp is a great idea, Patty, but unfortunately it's too late already," he said.

"What do you mean?"

"Well, it's just a couple weeks before Memorial Day now, and the town needs more lead time to get a new program up and running, you know, to promote it and generate attendance. There's just not enough time to have it in place for this summer."

Patty made a slight turn away from the sun. "Well...but we're good to go with the new 'Park Plan,' right?" she asked.

"The Park Plan." It sounded benign to anyone who overheard it, especially around Ronny. Patty started building the plan when they were together that night at Nero's a few weeks earlier. Working at the bank was just her start out of college, but she was anxious about where her Finance and Psychology degrees would take her. She wasn't sure that the City would be the right place. Her degrees pointed toward Wall Street, and many of her classmates were now riding the Metro-North train into the City on a daily basis, but her competitive swimming background pulled her in a different direction and an entirely different lifestyle, one with more sunshine and water. She felt she had to get out of small-time Connecticut, unlike the three friends she was with that night. David the accountant had been locked to his desk doing tax returns, drowning in a flood of financial figures. He looked like an old man already, aging in dog years. She saw no excitement there. Jennifer's working in a travel agency enabled her to pursue her passion for visiting new places, so it was a good fit for her. Talking to Jennifer reminded her how much she loved the Bahamas. Ronny was great with kids and running leagues. He was happier on the playing fields than in the office. Playoffs, lineups and team equipment made him smile. League insurance, umpire schedules and team registration fees made his eyes glaze over. Patty saw that as her opportunity, and possibly a shortcut to achieving her dreams. It was the genesis of "The Park Plan," and she needed him on board to pull it off.

Her *entrée* for some one-on-one time with Ronny was to pitch her idea of starting a Swim Camp. She was semi-serious about starting a program at the YMCA's pool teaching children an introduction to competitive swimming. She made him believe she wanted to use her All-New England credentials to help younger swimmers improve their strokes and strategy. In reality, the Swim Camp idea was a smoke screen to learn more about the inner-workings of the Parks & Rec. Department, and his role in the financial side of it, which turned out to be little more than running the checks to the bank on a weekly basis.

Their group of close friends visited each other's homes often, either individually or in various combinations. She started dropping by his house more often after dinner, while he was watching a ballgame on TV and before he'd go out for the evening. She went over one night when Jennifer and her mother were in the City. Ronny was sitting in the den when the Mets game went into a rain delay, so he turned down the TV and turned up the stereo, which sat on a shelf beneath a collection of shiny trophies. She saw that as her best opportunity to make her case. It was a conversation she had been rehearsing and refining in her head for weeks, so she was prepared for this moment.

"Ronny, I want to ask you about your office," she said.

"Geez, I'm off work now, what's up?" he said, more agitated about the baseball game being delayed than the question. She knew that and brushed it off.

"Well, I usually process your deposits at the bank. It seems like you don't know what the total is until I tell you," she said.

"Yeah, I'm not the bookkeeper. I figure they have that handled anyway. I just take the stack to the bank. It's a favor and an excuse to get out of the office. I've always done that," he said as he walked back and forth to the kitchen for a beer. He sat back down in his favorite spot on the end of the leather couch.

"But it's like they're not keeping track until you bring back the deposit slip," she said.

"Hey, I guess that's how they wanna do it. I've got league schedules and umpires, fields and maintenance. That's my area." He took another sip and put the bottle on a *Sports Illustrated* he was using as a coaster.

"I know, but there's a big opportunity here…for us," she said.

"What do you mean, *for us*?"

"It's an opportunity for *you* to get what *you* want, and for *me* to get what *I* want. I'm calling it 'The Park Plan.'"

She switched seats and sat on the opposite end of the couch, turning his vision perpendicularly away from the TV. In an excited tone, she said, "I've figured this out. Some of those checks, some *specific* checks, can go into a separate account. Your bosses, the Department, and the town will never know the difference."

He sat in stunned silence. She expected this reaction from him, so she waited for him think about it. After taking another swig of his beer, he said, "What are you talking about?"

"It's easy, but this is the important part. When you gather the checks and come to the bank, make sure all the checks made out to 'Greenwich P. and R.' or 'Greenwich Parks and Rec.' are on the bottom of the pile. We need checks with those names specifically, no variations."

"What?"

"Yes, just like that. You still get your deposit slip. It just won't be for the full amount. We've already determined your office doesn't keep track of the funds until you bring back the deposit slips. They have no idea how much money is coming across their desk, so some of that money is going into another account."

"What account?"

"It's an account I control but it's not in my name. It's a business account."

"What business?"

"It's better for you not to know, so in the slim chance you're ever asked about it, you've never heard of it before. The less you know about it the better it is for you."

"Whoa, whoa, hold on. Give me a minute," he said.

He picked up his beer and took another gulp as he walked across the den. He turned off the TV and turned down the music. He rubbed his finger across the nameplate on one of his trophies then lined it up with the others. Thinking and stalling at the same time, he finished the beer, took it to the trashcan in the kitchen and brought back another. Walking back to the couch, he saw her sitting with perfect posture in a sleeveless light blue blouse and a short dark blue skirt, with her legs crossed, one foot dangling and swinging a sandal back and forth. Her hands were folded in her lap, her head tilted up toward him, as she calmly waited for a response. He knew her idea was illegal, irresponsible and dead wrong. Still, he was captivated by her presence, personality, and presentation. Her sandal swinging back and forth like a pendulum on a grandfather clock marked the time until he answered. He visually followed that sandal up her long toned leg. He looked at her wavy blonde hair, green eyes, full red lips, and her extraordinarily large, luscious…dimples.

"It can't *possibly* be that easy," he finally said as he slid back down in the middle, not the end, of the couch.

"I believe it is. I *know* it is," she said quietly but firmly. "Everything I learned in Finance to what I've seen in the bank to what we know about your office's record keeping says so. There are *no* loopholes." She turned slightly toward him and kept swinging that sandal.

"But…I'll get in trouble," he offered.

"I don't see how," she continued. She had already anticipated this part of the conversation. "First, your name isn't on any account anywhere. You're just the courier for the office, an office that keeps its financial records after the fact. So really, there is no paper trail coming back to you, no *proof* you're involved. *I'm* the one at risk. It's *my* account and you don't know anything about it."

"Yeah, but what if something happens?" he asked, shifting on the couch and turning more toward her.

"Like what, *the police* finding out?"

He started to answer but caught himself. He rolled his eyes slightly and grinned sheepishly, realizing what she had said. He took another chug of his beer as she started talking again.

"C'mon, think about it, Ron. The big, powerful Chief of Police would surely protect his only brother if he got in trouble. He'd prevent him from *getting* in trouble in the first place. Don't you think he has a huge interest in protecting the family name? His *own* reputation? He wouldn't want that embarrassment, no way."

Ronny looked briefly at his trophies, then looked back at her and nodded.

"How about the *Mayor* and the *whole town*?" she continued. "They have so much at stake with your brother being such a big-shot. You know how this town is. It would *never* want any scandal or public relations problem leaking out, on the front pages of the *Post* and the *Daily News* again like Martha Moxley. They'd sweep that under the rug as fast as they could. And Mayor Bentley, he'd be humiliated. It'd ruin him and crush his political career." She went in for the kill. "Ronny, you've got the Mayor and the police in your back pocket and you don't even know it. You're bulletproof, Ronny, bullet-f'ing-proof."

Ronny was startled. It was the first time he had ever heard her swear. He had not thought about having any position with leverage that could be described that way, nor any previous reason to want it or use it. She sat back, confident she had made her case in a way he would understand and accept it, but she still had contingency plans. He subconsciously straightened and flexed his "bad" knee, rubbed it, and propped that leg up on a small pillow on the coffee table. She scooted half a seat closer but kept her sandal swinging back and forth, now nearly brushing against his leg. He took a deep breath as if he had reached a conclusion.

"Well, okay, I get all that. It sounds like a 'Bonnie and Clyde' movie, and they usually get caught."

Patty could tell his wheels were spinning so she said nothing. It dawned on him to ask the ultimate, obvious question, the last piece of the puzzle.

"So if I go way out on that limb, what's in it for me?"

Patty knew he would get around to that at some point. She didn't need Dale Carnegie's book, "How to Win Friends and Influence People." She was young, beautiful, athletic, and physically gifted...and she knew it. She had developed and mastered "The Look." It was an innocent-yet-not facial expression she had perfected over the years to wrap men around her little finger, especially when men were interested in more than just her little finger. It was a very convincing and effective trump card. She started rubbing his "bad" knee and broke out "The Look," which he had not seen from her until this moment.

"If I get what *I* want every Friday, you can have whatever *you* want every Tuesday and Thursday, all summer, I promise," she purred quietly. She moved even closer. His resolve diminished as she liberated each strained buttonhole on her shirt. He wanted to put his face in the place with the lace, and she knew it. He was lost in the moment, and lost in her cleavage, until he said, "Wait, what about Jennifer?"

She stared at him and said, "Who?" Five seconds later, she added, "She'll *never* know."

"I just don't know. The bank, my brother, my job, Jennifer…that's all so much."

She figured he might waver, so she took an extra step.

"It will be an amazing summer, and when it's all over, I will take us for a huge weekend on a tropical island far away from here to celebrate. Just me in a little white bikini on the beach, with you. All you have to do is say 'yes.'"

He looked up at her but couldn't muster a reply. She stopped swinging her sandal just long enough to swing her entire leg over both of his. In one graceful, fluid motion, she was now straddling his lap, facing him on the couch. She pressed into him and whispered, "Let me help you say 'yes.' I know you want to."

They sealed the deal. That night, Ronny dreamed he was swimming in the deep end, and Patty was the lifeguard.

Back at Binney Park, Ronny looked across the ball field, past the weekend athletes he used to dominate before his knee injury. He refocused and looked at her squarely in the eyes, which took some concentration.

"Patty, I don't know anything about it," he said with a sly grin. "I'll see you at the bank Friday, as usual." This last Friday of the month was the start of Memorial Day weekend.

"Good," Patty said. She was used to getting her way. In fact, she was counting on it, especially this time. She adjusted her sunglasses as they headed back to the bleachers. Most of the players glanced over again as Patty and Ronny walked together, the Swimmer and the Star. Two of Greenwich's greatest. Steven recognized Ronny and had no idea who the beautiful blonde was, but thought she was vaguely familiar.

"I have to go, Jen. More games to see over at the Rec. Center," Ronny said. "Call me after dinner." He gave her a kiss and left. Patty told Jennifer about the Swim Camp, and feigned disappointment about it being too late for that summer.

"Maybe next year," Jennifer said. Patty replied, "Yes," but she knew it was untrue. Shortly after that, the game finished. The YMCA beat Byram Builders 24-11. The girls walked closer to the team as they packed their gear.

"Good game, you guys. Where's the party tonight?"

The guys looked at Patty and Jennifer, then each other, and finally toward Mark. As one of the "Four Aces," Mark would know. Of course he did.

"We're gonna start with bowling and pizza with Alex at the Lanes, about eight, late dinner. It's Ladies' Night, you know," he said.

Patty looked at Jennifer and shrugged, indicating it was an option, not a decision. The guys, however, nodded approvingly and started recounting some of the big plays of the game, including a diving catch by Chris with the bases loaded. The next two teams were ready to move into the bench areas and start their game. Richard's Men's Clothing Store was on their side, and Bruce Park Tavern was on the third base side. Mark and a couple other teammates walked around to say hello to a few of the Tavern players. Steven felt uncomfortable about that, so he said "catch you later" to no one in particular, grabbed his bat from the backstop, and turned to leave. He already had plans for the night, and they didn't involve bowling.

"'Stretch,' whatcha' doin'?" Patty called out.

Steven stopped and turned back. It took a second, but he matched the voice to the face and he remembered who she was, and why she was vaguely familiar.

"Well, 'Queen Guppy,' it's been such a long time," he said. The nicknames triggered and confirmed who Patty was, and his response. He had spent a couple of summers as a lifeguard at the Greenwich Country Club. Patty was the star of the Club's swim team. He was a lifeguard, but most days he was somewhat like a camp counselor; Patty was part of a group of kids that was there almost every day—too young to work, too old to stay at home doing nothing. They were there even on cloudy days when the pool area was mostly quiet except for their own chatter and the radio playing in the guards' shack. Steven thought Patty and her friends moved together like a school of fish, so he called them "The Guppies."

"Patty? Patty Callahan? I don't believe it!"

"Yes, it's me!"

"Hey, do you remember Bill Withers and the 'I know' song?" he asked. "Ain't No Sunshine" was a huge hit that summer.

Jennifer giggled and looked at her friend quizzically. Patty lit up at the reference, her eyes opening wide as she covered her mouth in astonishment. She started counting on her fingers and saying, "I know, I know, I know..." just like "The Guppies" did together whenever the song came on the radio that summer. She trailed off around seven then said, "How many, twenty-four?"

"Twenty-six, I think."

"Wow, I had almost forgotten all about that. Oh, excuse me. This is Jennifer, Ronny's girlfriend."

Steven had assumed *Patty* was Ronny's girlfriend. "Hi Jennifer, how are you?"

"Fine, thanks. So, what's this 'Queen Guppy' thing all about?"

Steven smiled and looked at Patty before summarizing. "Oh yeah, that was kind of out of the blue, I'd admit. That was my nickname for Patty when she was on the swim team at the Club when I was a lifeguard there. Her friends were 'The Guppies.' They were there all summer long."

"Oh, that's funny."

Patty suppressed a blush and jumped back in. "I recognized your name in the paper," she said. "Those Tavern reports were really good." He reacted with a half-smile and a nervous glance across the infield.

"Thank you. Really it was just paying attention, staying organized, and putting the pieces together. The police did all the hard work."

"Well, you're a really good reporter."

"Thanks. So, look at you! Where did you go to school? Did you keep swimming? What are you doing now?"

Patty compressed several years into a few sentences, and told him about her two jobs.

"Maybe I'll see you at the Y now that I know you're there," he said.

"Okay, see ya!" she said, walking away confidently. The girls got back in Jennifer's gray Volkswagen Scirocco.

"So, you like that guy?" Jennifer said.

"Well, we'll see."

"Oh my gosh, he's *so* tall!"

They looked at each other and started giggling. Their conversation continued as they went to Jennifer's house, driving out of the lush, well-kept park. Jennifer glanced longingly at families picnicking, with their children tossing bread to the ducks and floating plastic boats in the pond. Jennifer promised herself that would be her life one day. Patty looked at the same scene and thought about how her future, maybe her near future, would be so very, very different. The car stereo played rock and roll, but Jennifer heard wedding bells and Patty heard Calypso music.

Those two pretty girls were on Steven's mind as he tossed his equipment into the trunk of his Cutlass.

"Yo Steve-oh!"

Another nickname, but this was more immediate. Chris turned down "Big Shot" by Billy Joel and leaned out the window of his dark red, 1971 Chevrolet Chevelle SS. It was his high school graduation gift, and he kept it in mint condition. "You goin' to the Lanes tonight?"

"Nah, I got plans so I doubt it. You goin'?"

"Yeah. Plus the Mets are in L.A. so I can watch them later."

"Good point."

"Thanks, see ya."

"Later, Chris."

Steven wasn't interested in Ladies' Night at the Lanes because he was focused on one lady in particular, and a dinner date with her in a few hours. It was a "meet you there" date, not a "pick you up" date. He wasn't counting on it being a romantic date, but he wasn't ruling it out, either. Regardless, it was one he had been looking forward to. He headed home to get cleaned up.

Chapter Eight

The Post Road covered the eight miles from Port Chester, New York, to Stamford, Connecticut. Tumbledown Dick's was near the midpoint, and only about a mile and a half from his house.

Steven left early enough to take his Cutlass to the car wash just down the street from the tan brick-and-shingle restaurant. Rather than sitting idly in a hard plastic chair in the waiting room next to the cashier, he preferred to walk along the glass windows, and watch his car go through the well-orchestrated process. He tipped the attendant and drove to the restaurant. A parking space had just opened up a couple of spots from the door, so he whipped around and backed into it. More often than not he found good parking places. His father said it was a family trait and he had no reason to dispute it. He thought he was the "par-King." He pulled open the oak and glass door and paused for a second, partly to "make an entrance" and partly to let his eyes adjust to the darker room. There was lively laughter at the bar. He recognized the source and wasn't surprised. Greenwich didn't produce many pro athletes, but Zeke Belton was one of them.

About twenty years earlier, Belton played ten years of pro baseball, including two seasons in the majors. He played alongside Mickey Mantle in the New York Yankees outfield during one of Mantle's MVP seasons. He also played for the Kansas City Athletics (the team moved to Oakland in 1968). Belton's first-hand stories about the Yankees in their glory days with Mantle, Yogi Berra, Billy Martin and Manager Casey Stengel, along with his pleasant personality led to plenty of free drinks around town. It also helped him become a respected referee in Greenwich, working the three main sports for the schools and summer leagues. The older men were enamored with the Yankees connection, while the younger guys, including Steven, knew him from refereeing their games. Zeke had refereed dozens of Steven's games at Greenwich Country Day when he played basketball for Coach French and baseball for Coach Wanko, and they became as friendly as any referee/player combo could be. When Steven got older, they even shared a few beers here at Tumbledown Dick's and other places, and became decent friends despite their age difference.

"Hey Steven," Zeke shouted above the crowd.

"What's up Zeke. Sorry, I got a date, I'll catch you later," he called back as he kept walking. Zeke waved and rejoined his conversation.

Steven's table was in one of the two parallel dining rooms. He took a seat on the far side of the table, facing the direction that he came from. The decor included bookshelves with old, leather-bound titles, so it felt like eating in a cozy library, which was just fine with the writer. When his date arrived the same hostess led her halfway back and then gestured in his direction. Steven stood up, pulled out the other chair with one hand and offered a one-armed hug with the other.

"Why, Miss Baker, so good to see you," he said. Tonight she did not look like Susie the Waitress, not at all. Subtract her ponytail, apron, and functional flat shoes, replace them with a version of the Farrah Fawcett hair, nice dress and heels, and Susie the Waitress was Sensational Susie.

He made a joke about taking a waitress to a restaurant. She laughed politely, gave her hair a slight flip, and scooted up to the table. They looked over the menus. She knew he was always nice to her at the Diner and the few other times she had bumped into him around town. She knew he liked her, and appreciated that he showed it in a polite and patient way. At the Diner she would skim the newspaper when a customer left a copy behind and take notice of his stories. A nice evening out was a rare treat for a hard-working woman like her.

A waiter in a freshly pressed white button-down shirt came by to take their order. Susie scanned the menu, scratched her right eyebrow as she decided, and chose seafood. Steven had already made up his mind for a steak and a baked potato, but he held his menu open until Susie was finished.

"How would you like that cooked?" the waiter asked him.

"By a skilled and sober professional," Steven deadpanned, with a gleam in his eye. Susie nearly did a spit-take with her glass of water and burst out laughing.

"In all my years as a waitress, I've never heard that one before," she said, reaching for her napkin.

"Me too," the waiter chipped in, chuckling. Steven smiled broadly and enjoyed the payoff of one of his favorite jokes.

They eased into a comfortable conversation. They had some mutual friends and they talked about their families. His grandparents were from Greenwich and Orlando, and his parents and siblings were in central Florida now, too. She said she grew up in Greenwich but now her parents and most of her relatives were in and around Westport and Wilton on the other side of the county. She said it was very helpful having relatives nearby because it was difficult being a single mother. He listened earnestly and intently. She took a deep breath and confided she had been a young bride with a baby when her husband was a soldier who went to Vietnam and never came back. A good life insurance policy and a fat government check paid the mortgage and did wonders, but those funds were gone and life was hard without him. She opened up about her struggles, but seemed upbeat and optimistic. He noticed that she maintained her composure throughout the difficult parts of the conversation. He was glad she shared that with him, but he also knew she needed a break from that stress, so he waited for an appropriate spot to redirect the conversation.

They talked about the 1976 Olympics—of course they admired Greenwich's gold medal skater Dorothy Hamill. Susie also said she liked gymnastics and swimming. "Mark Spitz back in seventy-two. We had a big crush on him," she said.

"Oh, you like swimming?" he asked.

"Love it, my whole family does."

"What about your daughter?"

"Wendy's a minnow. I think she has gills."

"Well, I have a pool. You should bring her over sometime for lunch and swimming. It'd be fun."

"Okay, that sounds great!"

"Good. You've already aced the evening wear, interview and talent portions, so only the swimsuit score remains for you to qualify for Miss America."

"Awww, come on!" Susie blushed but smiled from ear-to-ear, and they both laughed.

They talked about movies, television, music, and national and local news. She kept pace when he made various references, which pleased him greatly. Anyone who looked at them would have been surprised to learn they were on a first date. They finished eating and mutually declined dessert. She asked him about his most recognized stories, his reporting of the Bruce Park Tavern Scandal.

"Well, the fire's out, but I think the coals are still hot," he said. "You've heard of 'don't shoot the messenger,' right? The same guy is the owner and bartender there and he still doesn't like me much, so I keep my distance, and he keeps his." Steven left out the details about how he feared for his personal safety enough to receive a restraining order. He thought she had enough to worry about already.

"What do you mean?"

"The police and the state agencies did the investigating. I was just the reporter assigned to the story. I didn't uncover all the broken laws and trouble. I was the person who gathered the information and put it in print," he said modestly. "Those 'meatheads' don't seem to know the difference, so Castino and his cronies are still blaming me. They got in trouble, the police found out, I wrote it down, and somehow they're still acting like it's my fault. I used to love to go down to the Tavern for some shuffleboard and pizza, but now that's not such a good idea. The whole situation is still pretty ugly."

"Well, I guess we'll have to see what he does next, right?"

He nodded in agreement, and liked that she said "we." A moment later, a shared silence signified the end of their date. She excused herself, and said it was time to go. He smiled and said, "Sure, of course."

He knew she had to go back home, and she assumed that without saying it. They weaved their way out, turning some heads. They were a striking couple, even though they weren't one technically, but nobody else could tell any differently.

As they walked outside, she pointed toward her car. They went along the sidewalk toward it, holding hands. As they reached her light brown Dodge Dart, he went slightly in front, stepping down off the sidewalk into the parking lot while still holding her hand. Her high heels and his step down made them almost eye-to-eye. He smiled and said, "Tall guy trick. How does it feel to be over six feet tall?"

"I feel like I'm *ten* feet tall tonight."

She tilted her head back slightly. They had a long, warm kiss goodnight.

Once in their cars, they both drove south down the Post Road. As luck and traffic would have it, they wound up side by side at a red light at Indian Field Road. They made eye contact, sharing a "well, isn't this kind of funny" moment, then a smile and a look that seemed to cement their enjoyment of the evening. The light changed and they continued on, both happy for the evening they had, and the promise of others to follow.

*****

On the Friday before Memorial Day weekend, the Parks & Recreation office was buzzing with final preparations for the annual softball tournament. Nearly two hundred teams were coming from all over the Northeast. Plus, there had been a surge in beach pass applications by residents who waited until the last minute to gain annual access to Tod's Point and Byram Shore Park. Staff was swirling, the phones were ringing, and people were at the door.

"I'm going to the bank with this deposit then grabbing some lunch," Ronny announced. A few people looked up then went right back to work, not surprised because he usually made bank deposits on Friday afternoons.

Ronny took a fat envelope full of checks and made the short trip to Putnam Bank & Trust, as he had done many times before. This trip would be different, but he wanted to treat it the same, just like a playoff game when he was back in school, just like he envisioned it. He walked into the bank, stood in line then let an elderly lady cut in front of him. He wasn't just being polite; he was making sure Patty was his teller.

"Welcome to 'P B and T,' how may I help you?"

"Yes, just making a deposit," he said. "Greenwich Parks and Recreation Department."

"Very good," she said as she sorted through a stack of checks.

"Here you go," she said, returning a deposit slip. "Thank you for your business," she said cheerfully.

He smiled back and left.

Across the state line in Purchase, New York, an IBM computer buzzed and clicked as it managed the transactions from Putnam Bank & Trust and other financial institutions in the area. The computer nearly filled an entire room and had its own air-conditioning system. It was a state-of-the art "System/370" with a "Multiple Virtual Storage" operating system. In Greenwich, a few hours later and at three minutes before closing on the Friday before a three-day weekend, Patty handled a second batch of checks made out to "Greenwich Park & Rec." and "Greenwich P. & R." The massive computer ingested this information, processed it, and confirmed it by allowing Patty to print a deposit slip. Close to twenty-two thousand dollars had been deposited into the account of Greenwich Parking, Reconstruction and Resurfacing, a company connected to a Post Office box in Wilton, Connecticut, forty miles away.

Chapter Nine

On the first Sunday in June, Steven was enjoying a late breakfast at the Diner. He had been craving a Western omelet, but he also wanted to see Susie for the first time since their date. She would be coming in for a lunch shift. He figured that gave him enough time to read the Sunday paper and start its crossword puzzle while he ate and waited.

The local section had a huge feature story looking back at Memorial Day weekend and previewing the start of summer. There was a quarter-page photo of Chief Graham smiling and waving from the back of a red Cadillac convertible in the parade down the Avenue, and another photo of him throwing out the ceremonial first pitch at the softball tournament. The Chief was the town's most famous war hero since General Israel Putnam in the Revolutionary War. If he was uncomfortable being recognized for his military career, he didn't show it.

The article was by Thomas Clemons, a writer Steven knew fairly well. It summarized several of the town's events, and added look-ahead/prediction material from some merchants, town officials, and civic leaders. The story mentioned the softball tournament, which the YMCA had played in, winning two games before being eliminated. The story noted that 128 teams competed, with a team from Freehold, New Jersey, winning the championship. Steven was confused. He saw the bracket sheet at Binney Park and thought there were three groups of sixty-four for 192 teams, not two groups of sixty-four for 128. The tournament was played all over town, so maybe he misinterpreted the brackets, but felt certain the tournament was bigger than 128 teams. The story also quoted the town Traffic Engineer and a Parks & Rec. official saying attendance at Tod's Point was down five percent, but he didn't understand that statistic, either. Steven couldn't remember the weather the year before, but the previous weekend was gorgeous, and some people in his office who tried to go to the beach told him the line of cars at the main gate was backed up so far they quit and turned around. He liked Clemons and thought it wasn't like him to miss basic facts.

A photo of Mayor Bradley Bentley on the beach with a shovel, a bucket, and ten children took the center spot on the next page. Each of them held a scooped shovel-full of sand at the same time, spoofing those groundbreaking ceremony photos of adults wearing expensive suits and ill-fitting yellow hardhats posing with full-sized shovels. *Cute idea, whoever thought of it, and good P.R. for the Mayor, too*, Steven thought.

The next page had a small photo with an extended caption, showing Chief Graham shaking hands with now-Sergeant Danny Heaton. The Chief had promoted him and appointed him to lead an anti-drunk driving task force for the summer. Steven had been there for that brief ceremony. It was right after a usual morning briefing with the media, so it would get coverage. Heaton promised a "border-to-border booze battle." He said, "DWI isn't cool. We're going to put the 'heat on' drunk drivers."

The Chief had introduced Steven to Heaton then, and Steven told him he was amused by the alliteration and the pun.

"Thanks," Heaton said, shaking his hand more firmly than he needed to.

"Good luck this summer. I hope it stays safe and quiet around here," Steven said.

"Me too," Heaton said.

"Say… I might be interested in doing a behind-the-scenes story about DWI checkpoints. Most drivers just think they're a hassle because they're sober and it slows 'em down. I'd be curious to see what really goes into coordinating one, and it would be good publicity for the Department. It might sway more public opinion to your side. Whaddya say?"

The Chief and Sergeant looked at each other and nodded. "Seems like a good idea," Heaton said. "What do you need?"

"Can you just grease the wheels with a couple of your key officers so I can talk to them, maybe find out where some checkpoints will be so I can visit one in action?"

"Sure, we can do that," Heaton said. "I'll announce it to the whole division next time we have a staff meeting."

"That would be terrific. Thank you very much. Thank you, too, Chief." Steven headed back to his office, and thought about how he would juggle that into his schedule.

Steven was flipping through some "Dads and Grads" advertising when Susie brought over a fresh cup of coffee. Not a refill, but a fresh cup.

"No cream, no sugar, one ice cube, right?" Susie said. "I know how you like it."

He did a small double take as his mind raced for a witty rejoinder, but he came up empty. Score one for Susie.

"Well, that's good to hear, and I'm glad you do," he said, refolding and squaring away the thick newspaper. He had called her once at home during the week but she was busy and couldn't talk more than just a couple of minutes. She seemed relaxed and happy, which he took as another sign she thought their date went well. As she served some other customers, he looked up from his paper more than once in a while to see what she was doing. She topped off his coffee more than once in a while also.

"How's your week looking?" she asked. He knew that was a straightforward question, but like her opening line, it could be interpreted as more. He liked that. However, he cringed and rattled off some evening obligations.

"Oh, this week is a pain. The Planning and Zoning Commission is Tuesday night. That's always a late night, and the Representative Town Meeting is always a biggie. There's a new proposal about some sort of big parking garage downtown. I can't imagine where they'll put it. They're going to be debating part of the next town budget, even though the fiscal year doesn't start until October first. It seems like they just tweaked that back on April first. Four months, what's the rush? I'm getting a headache about it already."

"Well, good luck with that. If you want to cover entertainment instead of news, let me know."

"Oh really? For instance, what's playing at the Cinema?"

She scratched her right eyebrow and thought for a second, "Oh, I think it's that Clint Eastwood movie, but I'm not sure if it's still there."

"I'll drive by it and find out. Hey, what about the lunch and swimming that we talked about?"

"Let me check my schedule."

Susie popped open a small blue notebook she kept in her apron, then suggested, "How about a week from Saturday?"

"Good, that's good."

He paid for breakfast, rounding way up. He kept the crossword puzzle and left the rest of the newspaper on the table. He said, "See you later. I'll be around."

"I know you will," Susie said, smiling.

*****

"Good job you guys, tighten up those flip-turns and you'll be on your way," Patty said, smiling. She had accepted an invitation to be a guest instructor at the Club's swim team's practices. She felt compelled to help because when she was younger, there was no way her family could afford to be members. However, her best friend in school was also a member of the Club and the swim team, and that girl's mother was the team's assistant coach and a part of several influential committees there. Patty's friend's family sponsored and paid for her associate membership to boost the swim team. At the time Patty was simply excited to be with her best friend and to compete. Those summers also whet her appetite for the upper-income lifestyle.

Patty's name was still listed in several places on the big wooden board of pool records over by the guards' shack. That included the 200 Meter Individual Medley and the Medley Relay. The corner by that guards' shack is where

Steven usually leaned a chair on its back legs, listened to WPLJ and watched the pool. "I know, I know, I know," Patty started singing softly.

"What?" a young girl asked, looking up from the water.

"I know...you'll have a good season if you keep working at it. You're doing great," Patty said. The morning workout was just about over. It had been a stressful but otherwise normal week at work for her, but by Thursday night, she wasn't nervous about it. She planned to celebrate after the swim practice with some shopping at a few of the finer boutiques and jewelers on the Avenue. She freshened up inside the Club. She drove down North Street, turned left on Maple, and beat a yellow light to merge onto the Post Road. Steven's Cutlass was headed in the other direction at the same time, right there in front of the Second Congregational Church and a small hill full of flowers. A silver Datsun 280Z speeding down the Post Road caught his eye. Steven glanced in the rear view mirror as her car changed lanes and dipped out of sight. He felt slightly uneasy but couldn't quite place it. Maybe he was thankful it was a yellow light, not red. *Yellow, red. Where have I seen that before?*

*****

Up in Banksville, Mark wished he was feeling "slightly uneasy but couldn't quite place it." Instead, he was still full-blown uneasy, and the place was The Old Country House about ten hours earlier. Someone had the great-at-the-time idea to play tic-tac-toe with full shot glasses, loser drinks. Tic-tac-toe is usually a standoff when people remain sober, but there were few standoffs that night. By the time they were finishing, they were using the shot glasses to diagram football plays, eleven per side, with subs on the sidelines, even, and Mark thought his wishbone running formation was brilliant. Now he wished his head would stop pounding like a linebacker slamming into his helmet.

Mark had been up since the crack of noon. He made a promise to himself to cut back on the drinking...again. He let the warm shower wash over his head, hoping it might restore some of his memory of the previous night's activities. Bits and pieces of it came back to him. He knew it started at Bruce Park Tavern for the summer summit meeting of the "Four Aces." After sharing a pizza they drove up to The Old Country House. Frank was still upset about "The Scandal," angry actually, but knew he had to keep a low profile because of his probation and restraining order. It seemed he spent more time stewing over how to get even with Steven than he did finding ways to revive the Tavern's sagging sales figures.

"What if we get him to come up to Banksville, you know, across the state line?" Backcountry Bobby suggested.

"Yeah, that might work, if we can match up our work schedules so we're all off," Alex said, "but he likes to hang out in town, so why would he come up here?"

"I got it...softball," Mark said. "We can have our team's year-ending party here. That should do it, especially if he thinks a hot babe wants him to be here, and I can set that up, too."

"How you gonna do that?" Backcountry Bobby asked.

"Clubby, can you get me a handful of Gold Passes?" Mark asked.

"Of course."

"Well, there's this lifeguard at the Y; she is un-be-leeve-able."

"That chick?"

"Yeah, Patty," Mark said. "Anyway, she likes coming to our softball games, and for some reason she's been at Steven's heels, like a puppy. I can get her to do it."

"Really, *you*?" Alex asked half-seriously.

"Get over yourself, Romeo. I can make it happen, I'm sure of it."

The three men nodded vigorously at each other, then turned to Frank. He leaned back, rubbed a scar under the stubble on his chin, nodded slowly then silently raised a shot glass as a toast. The "Four Aces" clinked glasses to their new plan. That's what started the tic-tac-toe and the football diagrams. Around the same time at Bruce Park Tavern, the shuffleboard player had decided his course of action, set his sights down the board, and deftly released the puck off his fingertips.

Mark wiped the steam off the bathroom window and looked outside. His Camaro was parked reasonably straight in its normal spot on the edge of the driveway.

*****

Jennifer's lounge chair was reasonably straight in its normal spot on the edge of the back patio of her parents' house. She had turned it to face the sun and had been on the phone with Ronny. Her phone had the longest wall cable and handset chords Radio Shack had in stock, so it reached a good fifty feet from where it was plugged into the wall in the adjacent den. She was basking in the sun and also in the memory of her evening with Ronny the night before. They had been getting along quite well lately, and she was growing more confident their relationship was the real deal. She thought the idea of joining one of the town's most famous families was becoming more and more of a reality. She had allowed herself to daydream about her own wedding, and of course what an amazing honeymoon she could put together. She promised herself not to push him too hard, though. She sighed contentedly and skimmed through the Sunday *New York Times'* travel section.

*****

Ronny sighed and skimmed through the *Greenwich Time* on his kitchen table. There was a photo of his brother smiling and waving from the back of a red Cadillac convertible in the parade down the Avenue. He knew his brother's expressions and various types of smiles, and thought that one was phony. He looked at the other photo of his brother throwing out the ceremonial first pitch at the softball tournament. He remembered not long ago the newspaper ran a photo of him throwing a real pitch at the high school baseball state tournament. He used to beat his older brother in stickball and Wiffle ball growing up, but now Ray's in the paper throwing a pitch. *Well, there you go*, Ronny said to himself. *That's something else we can laugh about next time I see him.*

Ronny knew he and his brother had grown up quickly and in different directions since they used to play together with G.I. Joes and baseball cards. That seemed to be a fork the road for them, but he knew he wouldn't have been the player he became, the player he used to be, without Ray. He also knew times had changed, and it was important to keep his brotherly bond strong for their common daily interactions and also for the new "Park Plan" with its unlikely but just in case scenario. He cleaned up the breakfast plates and glasses that had been sitting in the sink half the day. He thought about his Saturday night with Jennifer. He also thought about his Tuesday and Thursday nights with Patty. He had never had a relationship like this one before. He didn't have to invest in its upkeep with phone calls, meals, movies, and real dates. She just showed up and was in devoted girlfriend mode right away, treating him like a king. Either later at night or in the morning, she was gone with a smile and a wave, like a breeze through the trees. He'd wake up some mornings, especially Friday mornings, and feel like the night before was just a dream, a very vivid, highly three-dimensional dream. A few hours later he would see her at the bank and they would act like strangers. That made it more of an amazing fantasy, one he was very interested in continuing while he was still seeing Jennifer. It was a terrific yet exhausting schedule when he was with Jennifer on Friday nights, too. He wondered if it was the best thing going, or a train wreck waiting to happen. He figured the breaks had swung back in his favor again, finally, and he deserved and would enjoy every bit of his good fortune.

Two days earlier, a good fortune of close to ten thousand dollars sped through banking computers and once again was routed to the account of Greenwich Parking, Reconstruction and Resurfacing.

Chapter Ten

June was a busy and exciting month. Local schools wrapped up and college students came home, energizing the town, especially at night. Camps and summer programs ramped up. Local government and the coverage of it were buzzing. In early June two meetings in the same week dominated the news and the coffee-break conversations. The Planning and Zoning Commission and the Representative Town Meeting shuffled and adjusted their agendas after Mayor Bentley announced plans to build a Greenwich Transportation Center, which he liked to refer to as the GTC.

The Mayor's announcement was a huge event by Greenwich media standards. The Town Hall occupied the former High School building on Arch Street just off the Avenue. Most announcements were just in the Mayor's office, but this one was moved to the conference center, which used to be the school's auditorium. The *Greenwich Time* was there in full force, along with several reporters from other nearby newspapers, and even a camera crew from a Hartford TV station. The Mayor was camera-ready, with a fresh haircut and a sharp pinstriped Perry Ellis suit from Richard's.

Mayor Bentley's vision of the GTC was a massive edifice near the train station close to the bottom of the Avenue. It would primarily be a four-story parking garage serving train commuters and local shoppers. The town would run shuttles, taking shoppers to and from the top and midpoints of the Avenue. The public-private project would not only house town-owned vehicles such as buses, vans, and snow removal trucks, but it would also have a centralized maintenance facility for all town-owned vehicles, including police cars and ambulances. It would also consolidate the headquarters of the taxi companies that served Greenwich. He said the location was ideal: near I-95, the Post Road, the train station, and the Avenue. The town would use town-owned property, purchase a vacant lot, and either buy or land-swap for a third parcel adjacent to both those properties. He said it would be the biggest improvement project in town since the new High School was opened nearly a decade earlier. Privately, he made a promise to himself to see this through no matter what. He thought it would be the crowning achievement of his tenure, his lasting local legacy, and perhaps springboard him into higher office in Hartford. He announced his intent to have all the ducks in a row by Labor Day.

The *Greenwich Time* wanted to not just cover this story, but to own it. The editors wanted to be aggressive and proactive, even if leads didn't pan out. They placed Steven and Thomas Clemons at the helm of a team of reporters that dissected the GTC from all angles: budget and funding, traffic and environmental impacts, costs and savings from consolidation, and retail shopping projections. An editorial pledged the newspaper would not just "cover and announce" the developments, but would "bring clarity and transparency to the entire process." That's why Steven was leading this reporting team. That was his strength. He did just that in covering the Bruce Park Tavern Scandal, the *Hartford Courant* buyout, and other stories.

He started a series of articles profiling the companies that may be involved. The first three included a firm named Parkitect that was the front-runner for the design of the project. It had developed several stadium, mall, and hospital garages in the northeast. Connecticut Concrete Solutions was an early bird. Byram Builders wanted in and trumpeted its local history. The articles took readers behind the doors of the companies, meeting key personnel, showing photos of previous projects, and providing details of their facilities and capabilities. Each article concluded by promising that more corporate profiles would follow all summer, including those considered long shots and smaller participants. "Nearly every company within three states involved with commercial construction, cement and parking would be contacted by the *Greenwich Time*."

Patty's jaw dropped when she read those words. There's no way anyone could have predicted this, at any level. "Greenwich Parking, Reconstruction and Resurfacing" was just a plausible parallel phrase. Might her little, imaginary company hit Steven's radar and become a target of scrutiny and exposure? That's not the type of exposure she was comfortable with. Instead of shutting down the "Park Plan," she launched a counter-move, along the lines of "keep your friends close and your enemies closer." She needed to know what Steven knew before it hit the newspaper, to perhaps *prevent* damaging information from being printed, and there was only one way to do that. She added Rollins reconnaissance to her list of tricking the bank, ensuring Ronny's continuing participation with her personal visits, and hiding those trysts from Jennifer.

Throughout the rest of the month, Patty attended every YMCA softball game, becoming the team's scorekeeper so she could sit on the bench. She spoke more with Steven before and after games, increasing the friendly-flirty chitchat and adding seemingly earnest "What are you working on?" questions. He didn't mind the discussions. She started going to the team's post-game meals and parties and crossing paths with him at the YMCA's gym where he still played basketball on Wednesday nights. Steven's articles and Patty's interest continued all month, until the Fourth of July when she went out of town for the weekend. He was flattered but discounted the attention. He assumed it was a rekindled version of their "Queen Guppy and the lifeguard" days when she was a kid, even though he was well aware she was no longer a guppy, far from it. Tempting as she was, which was *very* tempting indeed, he did nothing with her outside of his normal routine because he was still seeing Susie.

Steven was doing just fine with Susie, as a matter of fact. He understood her time vs. money situation, working hourly and for tips. Not working meant having no income, and possibly adding expenses. She liked to tell him, "When I win the lottery, I'm moving to the Bahamas." She told him once it was a long-standing family joke. She strove to find a balance. He realized that and was pleased to be a part of her equation. He helped contribute to the solution by visiting her at the Diner. She had been working some double shifts to prepare for taking a few days off to stay with her parents and to visit her relatives. They had clicked at Tumbledown Dick's and they started to spend more time together. They met for pizza at DaVinci's. Another time they took a stroll around the pond at Binney Park and played catch with a Frisbee. Eventually, Susie decided to take a big step and bring Wendy into the mix, so they arranged to meet at Baskin-Robbins downtown one evening.

Steven was coming back from a story when he asked the photographer to drop him off at the top of the Avenue instead of going back to the office. The Avenue was Greenwich's version of "the mall." It was a destination for kids flexing some newly found freedom, to get to roam until meeting a parent at a particular store at a predetermined hour. It was a place to learn about budgeting and personal finance, where young teens scraped together allowances to see how far a few bucks could go. People hung out there and dated there. It's where older teens and young adults saw real people working real jobs, and filled some of those retail shifts themselves. This one street opened all those possibilities and all those experiences.

Beautiful blooming trees lined both sides of the slightly downhill street. A small portion of Long Island Sound glimmered in the distance, offset by the clear sky overhead. All this natural beauty was contrasted by vehicular congestion and commerce: two great forces of nature and development blending and competing at the same time. It was a strong dynamic.

Steven went about fifty feet down the sidewalk and stopped at Putnam Barber Shop. From the time he was five until he was fifteen, he and his father would go there together for haircuts. Now that he was living in town full-time again, he started going back. He was comfortable there, and felt a combination of loyalty and friendship with the store's proprietor. Putnam Barber Shop was so small it almost had no storefront. A miniature barber's pole stood out front, and its name was etched in the door. Steven pushed the glass door open and immediately turned right and went down six steps.

"Big Steve, how are you?"

"Mr. Mike, good to see you again."

Steven has been calling him "Mr. Mike" since he was a little boy, and enjoyed keeping the tradition going. Mike started calling him "Big Steve" when he was just a kid, and now Steven found it ironic and amusing that now he actually fit the bill, nearly a foot taller than the older man.

Steven scanned an array of magazines and newspapers on the windowsill, which was below eye-level to him. The long, horizontal window was sidewalk-level along the Avenue, and its wide sill doubled as a buffet of periodicals. He grabbed an issue of *Sports Illustrated* with

Pete Rose on the cover and slipped into one of the five Naugahyde seats across from the five barbers' chairs. When Steven was a boy he'd listen to the men talking about a variety of topics, most of which he didn't understand or care about. He was more interested in the spectacle of men being shaved with straight-edged razors while reclining in the huge, black leather chairs. Now that Steven was older, and a reporter, he was much more interested and invested in these conversations (but he declined the shaves).

Mike was more than a barber; he was somewhere between an acquaintance and a friend for more than twenty years. He was also a valuable resource because he was in a position where he heard and participated in a lot of conversations, both factual and gossip, something Steven understood from his lifeguard summers. Mike would share what he knew when asked, but had mastered a tactful way to express it. Mike worked at the first chair, next to the cash register. Angelo was tidying up his area around the fifth chair, and the middle three chairs were vacant. Angelo didn't mind that Steven was waiting for Mike. In fact, he expected it. Mike's chair opened up and a few minutes later he was ready. Mike had spent his entire adult life there, and had saved enough money to buy the shop several years earlier. His same short hairstyle was now equally gray and black, and his small round glasses were a concession to his age. He occasionally clenched and unclenched his hands to improve his circulation and to stave off the effects of arthritis. Steven settled into the chair as Mike attached the gray nylon smock around his neck.

"Same today, Big Steve?"

"Sure."

Steve looked at the shelf full of carefully aligned scissors, razors, combs, powders, and other supplies. He watched in the long, horizontal mirror across from all three chairs as Mike began his handiwork, and then used the reflection to look past him out the window on the Avenue, where he could see pedestrians only from the waist-down and the lower halves of parked cars. Most of the front door was in his vision farther to his left.

Above the mirror was a row of framed eight-by-ten photos. The section on the left, above the cash register, was reserved for the High School's undefeated football teams. The series of photos included the school's first state championship team of 1946, the surprising 1953 team, another title-winner a decade later with the 1962 squad, and then a color photo of the 1974 Cardinals, in their bright red uniforms, a team that steamrolled everyone and set a league-record for scoring. Above Angelo's chair in the right corner and adding chronologically from right to left was a row of individual photos, starting with black-and-white photos of grizzled coaches with military crew cuts, ostensibly from those early title teams. A photo of a running back standing casually with a ball under his arm after he ran for a school-record 364 yards in a game in 1970. Next to him was Ronny Graham. He was in uniform but without a helmet, smiling broadly in a classic mid-pass pose, the ball cocked above his right shoulder and his left arm pointing downfield. The next photo was a candid shot of a coach hoisted on the shoulders of his players after winning the 1974 state championship.

Talking about the football team in a one high school town was as common as talking about the weather. Even though it was not Steven's school, he had no choice but to keep up with the Cardinals.

"Are you saving a spot up there for that quarterback we have now?" Steven asked, using the community "we."

"Yeah, you're probably right about that kid Young. Quite an athlete. He's on the baseball team now, and threw a no-hitter last week against New Canaan."

"I heard about that. I've been meaning to see him pitch. How would you compare him to Ronny?"

"Well, that's tough because Young's still a junior, but Ronny G, 'Ronny Gee Whiz,' his senior year he had only one interception, and that was on a deflection. He was in here last week, actually," Mike said.

"Ronny?"

"Yes. Ronny, a lot of those guys who are still in town like to come in here and talk football, especially in the fall."

"How's he doing?"

Steven knew what Ronny did, but had never actually met him. Mike finished up Steven's neckline and switched to scissors to start on the top of his head.

"He's good, Busy with the summer programs. Baseball and softball, you know."

"Right, I saw him at one of my games."

"Sure, well, he was on a roll that day he was in here. All pumped up and bragging about having two hot girlfriends, a brunette and a blonde. He said all he needed was a redhead to complete the trifecta. I'd like to cash *that* ticket," Mike chuckled. Angelo looked over and grinned.

"A brunette *and* a blonde?" Steven asked.

"Yes."

"Sounds great, but I don't think I could keep two girlfriends apart, much less *three*," Steven said.

The conversation paused as Mike worked through Steven's thick hair. Steven looked up as another customer came through the door and went over to Angelo's chair.

"Mr. Mike, what have you heard about Mayor Bentley's Transportation Center plan?"

"Well, the traffic engineer was in here. He seems to like it."

"Do you think he actually likes it or was he just toeing the company line?" Steven asked.

"No, I think he likes it. He thinks the shuttles will work."

"Maybe Ronny could use the shuttles for his girlfriends," Steven joked. "You gotta like the idea of vanloads of people being dropped off right here at the top of the Avenue, right?"

"Yes, it can't hurt. Haircuts are more intentional than spontaneous, but more foot traffic can only help."

"What about the rest of it?" Steven asked.

"Well, there's a lot to it. We'll have to see how the dollars line up and how the Mayor plans to pay for it. Maybe some corporate sponsors and grants?"

"Probably, but if anyone can take a project from the back of a napkin to ribbon cutting, it's Mayor Bentley," Steven said.

"Who's been interested?"

"Well, I've written about a few companies and am always working on others. As for locals, Byram Builders is pushing hard to get involved."

"Byram, with Peter Tosco?"

"Yep, that's him."

"Pete was in here, too. He saw your article and liked it. He said it might help his bid."

"Great. What else did he say?" Steven asked.

"He mentioned a company in the City. Lundgren, Loftberg, something like that. They made the toll booth gates in Byram on ninety-five."

"Okay, I'll check that out, thanks."

The conversation and the haircut finished. Steven paid and thanked Mike.

"Take care, and say hello to your father for me next time you call him."

"Will do." Steven waved good-bye to Angelo and climbed up the six steps to the street.

Steven took a deep breath of fresh air and continued down the Avenue. He stopped in Favorite Shoe Store to pick up a pair of loafers he had to special-order. While we was sitting on a sidewalk bench to take a closer look at the new shoes, a woman and her children brushed by and hopped into a car with out-of-state plates. The white-on-green license plate said Vermont but the mother's presence and demeanor said Greenwich.

"C'mon kids," she said as she pulled at her crisp, cardinal red sweater. "My old high school is right down the street."

The new Mercedes had tinted windows and was a model that was shipped from Germany and was not yet for sale in the United States. Steven recognized it from the cover of last month's *Car & Driver* back on Mike's windowsill. He watched its taillights blend into the traffic then disappear.

Steven crossed the Avenue at the next intersection and continued his short walk. He was wearing khakis with a blue Brooks Brothers dress shirt rolled up his forearms, no tie. Like all the other boys at Greenwich Country Day, he had worn a jacket and necktie to classes every day for seven years, from third grade through ninth, so since then he tended to avoid ties. However, at his school all the students called the male teachers "Mister" or "Sir" interchangeably, and that foundation of manners and respect was imbedded into his daily conduct and served him well. It's why he called the barber "Mr. Mike." He was leaning against a parking meter when Susie and Wendy appeared between two cars.

Susie had *not* come straight from work. She wore crisp jeans, white Tretorns, and a tight pink Lacoste shirt with a matching ribbon holding back a ponytail. She was holding Wendy's hand as they came up the sidewalk. Wendy clutched a Barbie doll in her other hand, and was dressed similarly to her mother—jean shorts, white Keds, and a pink t-shirt, but her shoulder-length hair bounced with each step as she kept up. Even Barbie had a pink plastic hair clip.

Steven sized up the situation, literally. He took two steps back and sat on the side of a green, wooden bench, chopping his height down to Wendy's level. Susie smiled as she figured out the unconventional but thoughtful move, and recognized it from the parking lot at Tumbledown Dick's.

"Hi there!" Susie said.

"Hi, how are you two doing?" Steven asked.

"Great. Wendy, this is my friend I was telling you about. Mr. Rollins."

"Hi," Wendy said.

"Hello, Wendy. I've heard such good things about you. What grade are you going into next year?"

"Third."

"Oh, I had such a great time in third grade. Tell me something, do you like ice cream?"

"Sure."

"What about Barbie, does she like ice cream, too?"

Wendy giggled and looked up at her mother.

"C'mon, let's go in," Susie said.

They ordered cones and came back outside to the bench. Wendy plopped down in the middle. Steven sat on the edge of the bench at an angle so he could see them both better. Wendy did a pretty good job keeping ahead of the drips of the vanilla ice cream, but she clutched onto some extra napkins just in case. After they finished their cones they walked back down the Avenue, mindlessly window-shopping, and in no real rush to leave. They slowed to look at the window display at the Dress Barn. Wendy pulled her mother's hand so they could stop and admire gems in the window of Betteridge Jewelers. Susie stepped up as Wendy pointed out a shimmering necklace.

"Oh, that's pretty, Mommy."

"Yes, it certainly is."

Steven stepped up behind Wendy to look over her head to see the necklace. It was indeed magnificent, and worth more than a new car. He put his hand lightly on Susie's back. His focus shifted and he looked at the reflection of the three of them in the plate glass window.

"Yes, it's quite beautiful," he said. They walked across Lewis Street to Susie's car.

"So, the weather looks good for Saturday," Susie said.

"Mommy said you have a pool," Wendy said.

"Yes, yes. Lunch and swimming on Saturday. Are chicken bites okay?" Steven asked.

Wendy looked at her mother. Susie nodded at her.

"Okay with me," Wendy said.

"Okay with me, too," Steven said. "Noon maybe?"

"Sounds good," Susie said. "And thanks for the ice cream."

"Sure thing. See you Saturday."

"Bye-bye," Wendy said.

"See you later," Steven said. He stood on the sidewalk for a moment as they drove away, then he walked back down the Avenue. A few of the businesses were still open. He passed Waldenbooks and Woolworth's then he went into DaVinci's to see if any of his friends from work might be there. He didn't recognize anyone, so he left and walked around the corner on East Elm Street, to the newspaper's parking lot.

Chapter Eleven

Little was left of the box of chicken from Garden Catering, potato chips, potato salad, and chocolate chip cookies. A red Igloo Playmate cooler was filled with Hawaiian Punch, Tab, and 7Up. Three red plastic cups sweated condensation on a table under a striped umbrella. Three towels were tossed across two chaise lounge chairs.

"Mommy, Mommy, look it."

Wendy jumped into the shallow end and churned across to the stairs. She gasped, wiped water off her face, and looked at her mother for approval.

"Very good, honey," Susie said.

"You're right, she is a minnow," Steven said. Susie didn't react, but she noticed he remembered that comment from their dinner at Tumbledown Dick's.

"I started her when she was really little. She loves it," she said.

"I can tell. It looks like she's having fun."

"We *both* are," she said. "Hey, Steven?"

"Yes?"

"Do you, you! Feel like we do?" She sang the lyric as she flipped her hair back.

"Good one there, Miss Frampton."

She smiled broadly at him before looking across the pool. Steven admired Susie watching her daughter then turned to see what Wendy was doing. She was sitting on the top step, talking to her Barbie as she made it do twisting and flipping dives that defied gravity.

"I like that. Now this time try to go a little higher," Wendy told Barbie.

"She's in her own little world," Steven said. He was standing chest-deep in the deep end. The bottom dropped off sharply to its deepest point a few feet away then rose gradually to the shallow end where Wendy was playing. Susie sat on the edge of the pool, dangling her legs in the water next to him.

"So tell me," she said making a slight sweeping gesture, "about your own little world here."

Steven did not talk very often about his family's background, but he was starting to feel close enough to Susie to do that.

"That used to be my grandparents' house. They owned this whole property and several acres down the hill. It was a cow pasture down there a long time ago. In the late sixties they sold that lower pasture to the town, and it was turned into playing fields and parking lots for the new High School."

"Wow, that's some prime property."

"And good timing, too. They didn't really need the land or the money, so that paid off debts for lots of my relatives... mortgages, cars, vacations, plus some college tuitions, including mine."

"That was very generous."

"Definitely, but Gramps and Granny never got to see me graduate from Missouri. They both passed away when I was a junior."

"I'm so sorry to hear that."

"Thank you. It was not a complete surprise, but it's always rough, you know."

She nodded and touched his shoulder.

"Well, in their will they deeded me this guest house and easement rights, which means I can use the driveway. I was their oldest grandchild. The will called for their house and land to be sold. I don't think my parents and uncles and aunts wanted it anyway; it's too big and they're happy where they are. So the proceeds were divided among them. They seemed to be happy to just put checks in the bank, but it gave my parents a boost to relocate to Florida, where my other grandparents are."

"I can see why that would be better."

"Yeah, no one minded that I got this house, as far as I know. It took me a while to get used to someone else living *up there*, though."

"So who's there now?"

"A banker and his family. He works in the City. Nice people, two little boys. They actually own this pool, but it's cool for me to use it. They don't come out here much, and I just stay away if they're here first. It works out okay. Sometimes they have dinner parties or birthday parties out here, and I've been invited to a few of them."

"Sounds like a nice arrangement."

"Yeah, he's a nice guy. I think he actually likes that I live here, kind of like extra security on the property. It might make him feel better when he's away."

"Have you been in the house since they moved in?"

"No, I haven't really been invited, and actually, I think I'd rather remember it the way it was when Gramps and Granny were there."

"Yeah."

The conversation paused. Susie leaned back on her hands and flexed her thighs to bring her painted toenails to the surface. She fluttered her feet gently, making ripples roll across the pool to where Wendy was surface diving for golf balls. Steven walked a few strides to the deepest part of the pool, where he was neck-deep then he turned around and came back next to Susie.

"What's it like living near the High School?" she asked.

"No big deal, mostly. I can't even see it except in the winter, and all the traffic comes off Hillside." He looked at the trees behind his house, which blocked his view of the school buildings. "You know, sometimes in the fall I'll be out here, or inside with the windows open, and I can hear cheering at the football stadium or a soccer field. It's weird; I have no connection to that school, but it's *right there*. I'm so close, but I'm not a part of it."

"I get that totally. I graduated from the old High School, not this one. I have no memories down there, so that's not mine, either."

Steven was looking back at her when he said, "And the thing is, I'm reminded of it everywhere I go. My ninth grade class at Country Day had about eighty kids, then going off to prep schools and colleges, we're all scattered. When I see someone I know, it's a surprise. The High School has what, almost a thousand kids in each class? If I had gone to the High School, I'd bump into people I know every day all over town. Don't get me wrong, my education was top notch, it got me to Missouri and back here, but socially, it's been a very different experience."

"How does that make you feel?" she asked. He looked at the trees again.

"Truthfully…a bit like an outsider. Not like a guest, or a stranger, but an outsider in my hometown. Does that make any sense to you?" He looked at her and waited for an answer. She looked straight back and gathered her thoughts.

"I feel that way too, sometimes," she said.

"Really? How's that?"

"Well, my social life since high school has been really different, too. I got married young, and she took care of the rest," Susie said, glancing over to the shallow end. "My friends wanted to party in Port Chester, not shop for diapers in Woolworth's."

She forced a laugh and continued.

"Now, Some nights at the Diner, look, I know people aren't going to confuse it with Manero's or someplace like that, but sometimes people are enjoying themselves, having a good time, and I'm just part of the background. I can see and hear everyone having a good time, but it's not *my* good time."

122

"That happens to me at work, too. I've been to places from the Governor's office to Belle Haven mansions, and had conversations with people I otherwise would never get to meet, but I'm only at their level for that moment because I'm carrying a pad and a pen. I've been in rooms where powerful, influential people are making multimillion-dollar decisions, but I'm not part of the process; I'm just observing it. I belong there, but with an asterisk. I'm part of the background, too."

"I get that, I really do," Susie said. She lowered her voice so Wendy wouldn't hear her. She was still diving for golf balls. He moved closer to hear her better and rested his forearm on the edge of the pool next to her leg.

"I'm raising her by myself, you know that. Sometimes there will be a Parents' Day at school or paperwork where you fill in the names of the parents. And of course Fathers' Day was last weekend. Families with two parents are in the park and in TV shows and ads. I'm constantly reminded of…my unusual situation."

She looked at the water, took a deep breath then looked back at him. "I can't let it get to me. I'm being strong for me, and strong for her, too. I have to keep everything as normal as possible even though it's not," she said.

Steven thought she might get emotional at that point, sharing such personal feelings, but then he realized this was a pep talk she had probably given to herself thousands of times over the years, and probably said it out loud to other people before him. With each time she said it, she believed it more and more, like the way the color of paint on a wall gets truer and truer with each additional coat. He recognized that as an important moment.

They looked at each other as seconds slipped by in silence. She lowered herself into the water and he extended his arm to hold the side of the pool, like a lane line. She put one elbow on the edge of the pool and held his arm with her other hand. Their touching had a calming effect on each other. Steven spoke first.

"I'm sorry. I shouldn't be complaining, or comparing, either. I'm so fortunate. Where I live, what I do, who I'm with today," he said.

"It's okay. I feel the same way." Susie looked at Wendy and squeezed Steven's arm little tighter. "Do you think we could be anonymous outsiders together?" she asked.

"Anonymous together? Hmm, that's a phrase."

"A phrase, and maybe a phase," she said, smiling a little at her rhyme. Then she turned serious again. "What we lack in volume of friends we can make up for in the depth of the relationships we do have."

"Depth?" he asked.

"Yes, depth."

He hooked his hand behind her shoulder and slowly pulled her off the wall. She resisted only briefly then shifted her balance to let him do it. She couldn't touch the bottom of the pool so she clung to his arm like a lifeguard's buoy.

"What happens in that depth, when you can't touch the bottom of the pool?" he asked.

"Well, you hold onto someone who can, or you swim."

"How do you know which one to do?" he asked as he continued to slowly walk away from the wall.

"You trust your instincts and judgment."

"Holding—you're trusting someone else. Swimming—you're trusting yourself," he said.

"Right, like I said, instincts and judgment."

She swung around and held his extended arm with both hands, floating on her stomach with her head up. He walked and pulled her right up to the shallow end where Wendy was playing on the steps.

"C'mon, Wendy, it's time to go."

"Aw, Mom, do we have to?"

"Yes, we need to stop in the store on the way home. And don't forget Barbie."

"Ohhh-kaaay."

"I don't want you to drive home in wet bathing suits," Steven said. "Please, go inside and get changed."

"Really? You don't mind?" Susie asked, but she was not surprised he offered.

"Of course not. The guest room is upstairs, first door on the right. There's a bathroom just past that. I'll wait out here."

"That's very nice, thank you."

"Thank you," Wendy echoed.

Steven stayed by the pool as Susie scooped up her canvas pool bag and led Wendy into his house. He busied himself by straightening the chairs and sweeping debris off the deck. He cleaned up the remainder of the lunches and walked it over to a trashcan by the garage. He pulled on a shirt, sat in a chair, and drank the last of the 7Up until they came out.

When they had arrived at lunchtime, Susie and Wendy wore their bathing suits underneath their clothes because Susie was not sure what to expect. Susie was happy to be able to change into dry clothes because they were stopping at the store on their way home. The screen door was closed, and the wooden door was open. The small kitchen was to the left, and they walked through the living room on the right to get to the stairs. Susie noted the décor was distinctly bachelor, but not dorm room. There was a matching couch and recliner, maybe from Macy's or Sears, and a big wooden entertainment center with a color TV, stereo equipment, and a shelf of records. A glass and brass coffee table had two newspapers, and copies of *Rolling Stone* and *The Sporting News*. The decorations were mostly framed posters and photos of palm trees and beach scenes. A couple of wooden model lighthouses sat on a bookshelf. Susie remembered Steven talking about Florida, and for a poolside house the decorations made sense to her. The living room had plenty of natural light and seemed spacious.

Wendy charged up the stairs with Susie right behind her. They found the guest room at the top of the stairs. Susie saw it was nothing special, with plain but matching furniture, a made queen-sized bed, and an alarm clock on the nightstand. An exercise bike with a very high seat sat in one corner.

"Mommy, I have to go to the bathroom. Where is it?"

"It's the next door. You go first then I'll go."

Wendy slid through the door and closed it. Susie went into the guest room and unpacked her bag, laying out their clothes and hairbrushes across the bed. Wendy came back wrapped in her towel.

"You start getting changed and brush your hair, and I'll be right back," Susie said.

"Okay, Mommy."

Susie left the room. On her way back, she paused, and took four quick steps the opposite way to peek inside Steven's open bedroom door. She saw a matching dresser and nightstands, like in the guest room. A king-sized bed, made, had a dark blue comforter and matching pillowcases. His softball jersey was on the top of a full laundry basket on the floor next to the closet. A small wooden desk with newspapers and notepads was in one corner near a window that looked out over the trees. Above the desk hung his Missouri diploma and a photo of him in his mortarboard and gown with two people who had to be his parents. She thought the other photos on the walls looked like family at formal gatherings or vacations. She noted there were no photos on his desk or nightstand, in particular, no girlfriend shots or couple shots either there or downstairs. Instincts and judgment were good, but instincts and judgment *confirmed* were better. She padded back down the hall and joined Wendy in getting changed.

Wendy came bouncing outside first. Her hair and Barbie's were both a little damp and tangled. Susie had spent a bit more time brushing her own hair to make it look nice.

"Well, that was delightful," Susie said, hiking her pool bag onto her shoulder.

"I enjoyed having you both here. I hope you didn't get sunburned."

"Oh, we're all right. Everything is just…right."

"Thank you for having us over, Mr. R.," Wendy said in a prompted but genuine manner. She ran up and hugged his leg. Steven smiled at Susie, then reached down and patted Wendy on the back.

"You and Barbie can come over again, as long as your mother brings you."

Susie came over for a hug of her own and to pry Wendy loose. She didn't try very hard to pull Wendy away while she was hugging Steven. He could smell the chlorine in Susie's hair plus a hint of residual shampoo.

"We'll see," she said. "C'mon, little girl, it's time to go."

Susie and Wendy waved out the windows of their car as it curled past the multi-car garage and disappeared behind the banker's house.

Chapter Twelve

Steven had no great plans for the Fourth of July weekend, especially with Susie out of town. She told him she'd have him over for dinner after she returned. He went to the Friday morning police briefing, worked at his desk on some deadline stories until lunch, then spent the afternoon starting on a new assignment. A "Life in the Next Decade" Special Report would include articles along with ads from companies associated with the topics. The writers felt like they were preparing advertising and marketing copy without attribution, so they weren't too excited about doing the anonymous work. Steven and the others barely talked about it; they just wanted to get it done and move on to what they considered "real" stories. The Special Report would include articles about emerging technology, such as home alarm systems, audio cassettes being replaced by compact discs, and the ability to do banking from home on personal computers. He was aghast about cassettes being phased out. He chose the home banking story because he thought it would be the easiest one to complete. He picked up the phone and dialed the number of a banker in the City from memory. Yes, his neighbor. No attribution? No hassle.

On the Fourth of July, Steven sat in his poolside lounge chair and had a fantastic view of the fireworks show just down the hill on the High School's fields. Sometimes he'd have friends over for the Fourth, but he didn't feel like being a host this year. He needed a night out but had no plans. He figured the Indian Harbor Inn would be a good bet on a warm summer night. It was also the kind of place where he might run into some of the people he knew growing up, and that's exactly what happened. Twin brothers who he used to play golf with were there. Senator Webster's son was there with a foreign model attached to his elbow. Steven ordered a Molson Golden Ale and found a choice seat on the deck to enjoy the evening. As he did, a man walked down the hall and plunked a quarter into a payphone before dialing a number.

"I'm at Indian Harbor. He's here," the man said. The person on the other end said only "thanks" and hung up. Similar calls then zipped between Bruce Park Tavern, the Bowling Lanes, The Old Country House, and a private residence in Banksville. It seemed Patty wasn't alone in having "Rollins Recon." Delegates of the "Four Aces" were called for support. These delegates were not-coincidentally all young males, and least six feet tall and two hundred pounds. They enjoyed free beer at certain establishments in exchange for their flexible hours, reliability, and physical presence.

An hour later, the Indian Harbor Inn was in the "sweet spot." The remaining happy-hour/evening crowd was well lubricated, and the late-nighters were just starting to arrive, freshly cleaned up and enthusiastic. One of the

"Four Aces," two top "Kings," and several delegates were there. They were circulating casually, waiting for more information, a specific instruction, or an opportunity when two uniformed officers of the Greenwich Police Department came in and slowly walked toward the manager seated along the back rail. The manager wasn't surprised or upset. Several bar owners had been notified that as part of the anti-drunk driving initiative, officers would be making occasional "courtesy visits" throughout the summer. The idea was to provide a visual reminder of the consequences of drunk driving. Sgt. Heaton believed that seeing police in a bar deterred people from having "just one more." That decision might save lives, which would be better than dealing with making arrests, or worse yet, auto accidents. Most of the partiers watched curiously as the officers made a slow, deliberate loop of the vast deck, right past the main bar, and back out the front door.

Steven noticed the task force in action and couldn't ignore a potential story when it was presented right in front of his face. He said a quick goodbye, apologized to his friends and timed it so he left the Inn with the policemen. He caught up to them in the parking lot.

"Excuse me, officers, I'm Steven Rollins, *Greenwich Time.*"

The officers turned warily.

"Rollins, is it?" one asked.

"Yes, Steven Rollins. Good work back there."

The officers said nothing, waiting for Steven to continue.

"I won't keep you long. I had a meeting a while ago with Chief Graham and Sergeant Heaton about doing an article about the DWI Task Force."

That was the key to the lock. The officers recalled a previous staff meeting where his name was mentioned, and they made the connection. They both relaxed and stepped forward.

"Oh yes, now I remember. The Sarge told us about you. I'm Officer Federici," he said, extending his hand.

"And I'm Officer Bittan," said the other.

"Please to meet you both," Steven said. "Here's the short version. Checkpoints have a bad rap with the public because most drivers are sober and it slows them down. I want to do a story showing the *good* that checkpoints do, and use some local and national stats, try to change the image and perception. I'll show the benefit of your hard work in real life terms. It'll be pro-police, make *you* look good and the whole Department look good."

"I like it," Federici said. "How do we do this?"

"The checkpoints are usually late on Friday or Saturday nights, right? I'd have to know when and where some are so I can visit one or two. How do I do that?"

"Well, since the Sarge already signed off on it, you should be able to call in and the Coordinator can look at the schedule and tell you what's coming up," Bittan said.

"He'll give that information out?"

"For you he will since the Sarge told him about it. We'll talk to him when we get back to make sure. Just tell him you want to work with us," Bittan said.

"That would be terrific. Thank you, Officers."

"You're welcome," Bittan said.

Steven drove out, following the taillights of the police cruiser. A man who had been smoking a cigarette in the parking lot went back inside to tell his associates what happened. Some of them shook their heads and swore, calling him various names preceded by "lucky-." Phone calls went out from that same black payphone to three numbers, where men had been waiting for a report. All of them were disappointed, most notably the man at Bruce Park Tavern.

The Tavern was having another awful weekend, as it did on Memorial Day and most weekends since. It kept its hardcore and walking distance customers, but most people had chosen not to return, or simply preferred to stay at the new places they found while the Tavern was closed. The aftermath of "The Scandal" hung in the bar like a cloud of cigarette smoke and stuck to its shoes like spilled, dried beer. The first two summer holidays were disasters. There was slim hope, but no real reason to believe July and August would be any better. The man hung up the phone, and put down the beer mug he was drying. He stood motionless for a second, imagining someone's face on the side of the mug. He lifted it and threw it against the door to the restroom. The glass rained down on the linoleum floor and the sound thundered out of the corner. Only three customers heard it, and none of them did more than flinch. The man promised himself to do something about it...soon. He watched a shuffleboard puck track its way along the long, wooden surface toward the red and blue pucks positioned in the scoring area at the other end.

At the Indian Harbor Inn, the representatives of the "Four Aces" folded their hand. The game was over for the night, but it would be a long, hot summer.

Chapter Thirteen

The series of articles about the GTC created a buzz in town, so the editors cleared the decks of the reporters assigned to it so they could continue with greater focus. Steven and the others worked hard to stay on top of and ahead of all the news. His most recent article was about Lofgren Industries. The Brooklyn-based company was the biggest name in its niche; it made the booths, ticket machines, and gates used at the entry and exit points of parking garages and other protected property. The entrance to Tod's Point was built by Lofgren. The company also made the equipment for highway tollbooths, including the one on the state line in Byram on I-95.

Steven had been using his connections in state government from his Hartford days to sift through business listings, tax records, articles of incorporation, even telephone and postal records. He went after all the public records he could get his hands on, and drove himself cross-eyed skimming long lists for key words, such as construction, contractors and garages. That diligence led to a few articles, several phone calls that went nowhere or fizzled out, and some dead-ends. One such dead-end was a one-line reference to Greenwich Parking, Reconstruction and

Resurfacing. He was intrigued and thought it was odd a company named "Greenwich" was in Wilton. He called an operator, but there was no phone number listed for that name in Wilton. He kept pouring through the data. His next article was about the catering companies vying for the contract to feed the hundreds of workers who would be at the construction site.

*****

Susie was preparing dinner for three. She was slightly anxious about having Steven over for dinner. It was a big step for her to invite him to their house, even though they had been to his house already. Soon enough, his arrival melted those anxieties. He was carrying one large arrangement of assorted roses, and a smaller arrangement of daises and sunflowers. He also had a newspaper to show Wendy what he did, and he smiled when he noticed they already had a copy on their coffee table. He looked at her leftover schoolwork from June, talked about her best papers that she saved and looked at some of her drawings. Susie was cooking chicken on a charcoal grill in her small but neat backyard. A cute little Lhasa Apso named Rosie scurried around beneath her feet.

"Wendy, could you set the table please?" she asked.

Wendy and Steven both stood up. She straightened up her school papers as he folded the newspaper and placed it on the kitchen counter next to the telephone and a stack of mail. On top was a letter addressed to Susan Callahan Baker, with a return address of Mr. and Mrs. J.B. Callahan in Wilton, Connecticut. He paused and soaked it in. *Callahan? Wilton?* He thought about the two familiar names. She had mentioned Wilton during dinner at Tumbledown Dick's, but when she said "Westport and Wilton," his concentration ricocheted at Westport, where he once bumped into Paul Newman and Joanne Woodward while shopping. He was going to inject it into their conversation, but she had moved on and he didn't want to double back and be a name-dropper. Then he remembered the last time he heard "Wilton" was while he was researching the GTC stories. *Greenwich Parking and…in Wilton? Reconstruction…Resurfacing. Wilton,* he thought. He made a mental note to check his files at his desk.

The Callahan connection was more obvious. He casually took a closer look at some of the framed family photos in the living room and entrance hall. A few were taken before Wendy was born. One showed a young Susie with her parents and what looked like her younger brother and even younger sister outside the huge, wooden Dragon Coaster at Playland Amusement Park in Rye. All three were tan and squinting in the sun. He had seen that youngest face before, several times before, tan and squinting in the sun. It was at the Greenwich Country Club pool; he was positive about that.

Steven was upset with himself for not recognizing he had been spending so much time with sisters. He rolled his head back and looked at the ceiling. There had to be a reason, and he had to be careful approaching it. They enjoyed a wonderful dinner of grilled chicken and corn on the cob. Susie was sipping a glass of wine as Steven encouraged her to talk about her family. She had recently seen them for the Fourth of July weekend.

She said her younger brother Sean moved to Dallas after college. Her youngest sister Patty was also in Greenwich, but they had a drastic fallout. She explained how Patty was very busy with swimming, and when she had her baby Patty became even more self-absorbed and distant to her. As Patty became more involved with boys and went off to college, the less she cared about, or even asked about, Susie and Wendy. Susie reached out to her, but Patty would never return her calls or come into the Diner even though it was in plain view from the bank and the Y. Eventually she stopped trying. Susie said she was surprised to see Patty at their parents' house in Wilton. She thought her parents did it intentionally to help them work things out.

"Well, it didn't work out, and it was a very awkward weekend. She avoided me and Wendy and she left without even saying 'goodbye.' She's got some great banking job. At the picnic she was wearing huge diamond earrings and an expensive designer dress..." Her voice trailed away as she looked at the faded, second-hand couch in her modest living room. She took another sip of wine. "Well, Patty's been getting the 'red carpet treatment' for a long time. Swimming, boyfriends, now this job. Good for her, I guess."

When Steven heard about Patty being a swimmer, he knew for sure it had to be the same Patty Callahan.

"Did you have a good time swimming last week, Wendy?" Steven asked, changing the topic.

"Yes! That was fun, and when I get a little bigger, I want to learn how to dive and do flips off the board," Wendy said.

"I did my first back flip when I was ten, on vacation in Orlando," Steven said then turned to Susie. "I saw a photo in the hall with palm trees. Is that in Florida?"

"No, the Bahamas," Susie said. "We went there three years in a row when I was in high school. The greatest vacations ever. You've heard me say, 'When I win the lottery, I'm moving to the Bahamas,' right? Sean and Patty do that too. It's a family saying now."

Steven nodded. "Wouldn't that be something?" he said. "Here, let me help you with the dishes."

He felt badly about not telling her he knew Patty. It felt like lying or cheating, made worse because he cared about her; but in that moment, he decided to withhold the information a little bit longer. His instincts told him to wait for the right time to bring it up.

After Wendy went to bed, Steven and Susie enjoyed some quiet conversation on the back deck.

"So, what's going on? Catch me up," Susie said, as she curled both her legs underneath her on the padded chair.

"Well, my Fourth of July was better than yours, but not by much. I met some old friends down at Indian Harbor for some drinks."

"Anyone I know?"

"The Boutelle brothers from school."

"Sorry, no."

"Anyway, I also talked to some policemen there. It looks like I will be doing a story about DWI checkpoints."

"Good thing I'm not driving anywhere tonight," Susie joked.

"I'm not worried about you. And, softball is good. We lost to Richard's, but we're still in third."

"That's good."

"Speaking of softball, I have to ask you something."

"About softball? Okay…"

"What's your maiden name?"

"That's a softball question? Well, it's Callahan."

Susie shifted in her chair and furrowed her brow, unsure of where this was headed. Steven nodded reassuringly and smiled, then said, "I have to be honest about this. Your sister Patty, because she's a lifeguard at the Y, she's been coming to watch some of our games. She recognized me at Binney Park. Quite a coincidence, huh?"

Susie opened her eyes wide, then curled up tighter and took a bigger sip of her wine.

"You know Patty? Why didn't you tell me before?" she asked.

"I didn't put two and two together 'til tonight," Steven said calmly. "You've always been a Baker to me. I've had no reason to think otherwise."

Susie nodded and sank back into her chair. "Well, I guess you're right."

Steven felt confident he could put the next card on the table. "And in the spirit of full disclosure, there's another coincidence. I was a lifeguard in the summers at the Club when she was on the swim team there, so I remember her from when she was a little kid."

Susie sat with a blank expression, trying to absorb this new information. She was not on the swim team, and even though she did attend some swim meets to watch Patty, she had no reason to remember a lifeguard there. Steven gave her a moment to gain her composure as he swirled the ice cubes around in his glass.

"This is a lot, all at once," she said.

"I know, I'm sorry, but I felt I had to tell you."

Susie sat quietly a bit longer, then said, "That's it?"

"Well, yeah. Like I said, she comes to our games, and I wanted you to know because that would make it uncomfortable for you if you wanted to come see me play. But, of course she doesn't know about us."

Susie's eyebrow twitched when he said "us," but she took no offense to the usage.

"Soos, I know you don't get along with her, and I'm sorry about that, but that's got nothing to do with you and me. I'm all about my Miss Baker, you know that."

Susie smiled and readjusted her legs underneath her. "Yes, Mr. Rollins, you're right about that. You're here for me now, and I really appreciate that. It's almost like that part of my life is over. I'm more interested in spending time with you now than with *her*, anyway."

He raised his glass in a spontaneous toast. Susie finished her glass of wine. Steven felt relieved that he told her the truth and that she accepted it so well. For a minute they listened to the birds and crickets, and enjoyed the breeze coming across the deck.

"You've made a good impression on Wendy," she finally said.

"She's a great girl, just like her mom."

143

Her eyes twinkled under the stars. When it was time to go, he said, "It will be quieter if I just walk around this way," meaning through the back yard and the side gate, instead of going through the house.

They walked across the deck, and as he took his first step down, she put her hand on his shoulder and turned him around, like outside Tumbledown Dick's. She wrapped her arms around his neck and shoulders. He rubbed the small of her back as they shared a long kiss. As he walked around the corner, she looked at the stars and made a quiet promise to herself.

Chapter Fourteen

On a Monday morning, Steven was already at his desk at eight o'clock. He pulled the GTC file out of his cabinet and spread it out across his desk, leafing through the papers until he found the single-line reference to Greenwich Parking, Reconstruction and Resurfacing. Wilton was a much smaller town, with a population of about fifteen thousand people. This was the only business in Wilton with "Greenwich" in its title. His records showed it was the only business in the state with "Greenwich" in the title that did not have a primary address in Greenwich or Stamford. He called the operator again, but still no number. He sighed, grabbed the glossy red Parkitect brochure, and leaned back in his chair. He was looking at photos and diagrams of the parking garage adjacent to the basketball arena and Civic Center Mall built in Hartford a few years earlier when his editor called him into his office. Steven flopped the brochure back onto his desk and went into the office where they discussed the progress of his home banking story for the Special Report. Steven told him he was nearly done and was going into the City that afternoon to interview the banker to finish it up.

He picked up a white Styrofoam cup of newsroom-strength coffee on his way back to his desk. As he started to put away the GTC file to do some prep work for his interview, he looked at the Parkitect brochure again, which lay diagonally across the other papers. Beneath it was the listing he found before calling the operator in Wilton. He stared at the brochure and the semi-obscured sheet of paper underneath it. Of the line "Greenwich Parking, Reconstruction and Resurfacing," all he could see was "Greenwich Parking, Reco." He stared at it, took a sip of coffee, and nudged the brochure just a hair to the left. Now the paper read "Greenwich Parking, Rec." He drummed his pencil on the stack of papers and gave that phrase a long look.

License plates, crossword puzzles, number sequences, word and letter patterns, puns...they all caught his eye and triggered his interest. In his mind, he toyed with the name and eventually translated "Greenwich Parking, Rec" into "Greenwich Parks & Rec." Because he was an avid softball player, he knew a little bit about Parks & Rec., probably more than most other town Departments. He remembered reading the Sunday paper the Diner in early June. That morning he had questioned the size of the Memorial Day Weekend Summer Softball Celebration that he played in, finding the numbers to be under-reported. He also remembered thinking the attendance at Tod's Point was under-reported, too. He shrugged it off at the time. Now he was wondering...*Was that bad reporting, or good reporters being fed bad information? If so, who's benefiting from under-reported attendance figures, and how?* His instincts prompted him to request a copy of the latest attendance records at

Tod's Point. As for Greenwich Parking, Reconstruction and Resurfacing — in Wilton, no less — he thought, *Can this business be making any money without a phone number or a street address? Maybe it's a coincidence, maybe not...or maybe what used to be a dead-end in the GTC reports might be reopened in a whole new way.*

After lunch, he headed to meet his neighbor, the banker, at his office in the City so he could finish writing the "Living in the Future" Special Report more authoritatively. The banker split time between his main office and a smaller satellite office in Greenwich. Steven did a crossword puzzle on the express train into the City, followed by a short taxi ride to the office building. Steven explained the scope of the Special Report, then it was his turn to listen and jot down notes and quotes as the banker gave him an overview, including the time saving benefits and how easy the program was to use. Steven received a show-and-tell to better understand how it worked. He was impressed but not overwhelmed. Not so surprisingly, he started to get it.

"So, I could put my name in here, and if I had an account, it would print out the history?" Steven asked.

"Yes indeed."

"May I try it?"

"Sure, of course." The banker was pleased to be helpful and to be getting some attention in the local newspaper. He thought it might be good for business and make him more prominent in their affluent community. It also showed that he was on the cutting edge of new banking technology, which could only be a benefit to him and the bank. Within a minute, Steven's personal banking history came out on a printout, dating back to a spring day when an eleven-year-old boy walked in with his father and co-signed a passbook savings account.

"May I try a business name, for another story? It's just to look, not for print, and strictly off the record," Steven said.

The banker shifted from side to side on his wing tipped loafers, weighing the potential breach of privacy against increasing the chance of claiming a hefty portion of the vast untapped wealth in Greenwich.

"I'm not sure, but you know what? I just remembered I have to check on an account with my secretary at her desk." He walked to the door and turned back to him. "I'll be back in a couple of minutes, probably not less than two minutes, I'm pretty sure. So we'll pick this up when I come back."

Steven understood what he said and what he was implying.

"Yes sir, thank you," he said.

The banker left the room and casually flipped the door closed behind him. Steven had to think almost as fast as the IBM. *A free peek at corporate finances? A gift. Who? Byram Builders? Parkitect? Connecticut Concrete? Wow. What about*

Bruce Park Tavern? Hmm. Then he decided. *One shot - long shot. Greenwich Parking, Reconstruction and Resurfacing.*

The computer processed the request. He was lucky the account matched up, and the bank records came back quickly. It showed a somewhat new account with about ten deposits, a few withdrawals and one transfer. The dates of the deposits were spaced a week apart, all for around ten thousand dollars each, with a fat deposit in the end of May and even larger one in the beginning of July. He hastily scribbled down dates and figures in the back of his notebook, hustled back to his seat, then took a deep breath and looked at those dates. The first of June was on a Friday that year—Steven was paid every other Friday, so technically that was a three-paycheck month. The dates registered with him and a quick look at the calendar on the banker's desk confirmed it. Sinking back into the leather chair, he regained his composure, and tried to predict what would happen the banker returned.

An image of himself standing behind jail bars flashed through his mind. Clearly, he was not authorized to use a bank's computer. Had he broken some sort of state or federal interstate commerce laws? He had no idea what financial privacy regulations were squirreled away inside some leather-bound volumes in an attorney's office. He really didn't want to find out, either. He had gone out on a limb, even though he thought it was a sturdy one. The image of jail faded as he reminded himself it wasn't Chrysler's or Coca-Cola's financial secrets that came spewing out, so it shouldn't have raised any red flags. The banker left him alone in the office, which could be construed as some sort of negligence on his part, but he did it on purpose, betting nothing major would happen. They both needed each other and used each other at this moment.

We're in this together, and we're neighbors, too, he thought. Just play it cool.

Steven stood and walked across the office to look at a painting of a small brick lighthouse sitting above a rocky cliff, backed by a dramatic sunrise or sunset. Nothing gave away its location, but it was both desolate and beautiful at the same time.

The banker came in expecting to see Steven in the chair then turned his head to spot him in front of the painting.

"You like that?"

"Yeah, I've always had a thing for beaches and oceans, but generally more tropical than this. Where's this from, Ireland?"

"Massachusetts actually, Martha's Vineyard."

"Oh, you go up there every August, right?"

"Yes, we're looking forward to it."

The banker ripped the top sheet off the printer as he walked back to his desk. He gave it the once-over and saw nothing worthy of headlines at *The Wall Street Journal* or big enough to rattle the Securities and Exchange Commission. He placed it upside-down on his desk as if it was routine business and remained standing. Steven didn't show any reaction either, and asked him some more about his family's trip to the Vineyard, and told him about the one time he visited Nantucket. They compared the two communities before Steven thanked him, told the banker he'd save him a copy of the article, and let himself out. While he rode the train back to Greenwich, he was relaxed but energized, knowing he had everything he needed to finish the Special Report, and then some.

Steven didn't go to the town's beach at Tod's Point very often. A few times each summer it was worth the drive and traffic to see and be seen, and to get some sand between his toes. He could do neither of those at his pool. He had thought about asking Susie to go with him, but he knew she was working. Tod's Point was busy, as expected. As he pulled up to the main gate, he noticed it had a Logfren logo. He showed the attendant his media pass, said he was working on a story, and would be back later. A family was piling into a brown Chrysler Town & Country station wagon in a choice parking spot as he drove up. He waited a minute then backed in. A peloton of serious bicycle racers whirred past him in the parking lot. The reigning female champion of the Tour de Greenwich led the group on its training ride.

It was low tide on Long Island Sound. Some children played in the small pools on the exposed sandbars while others splashed in the small waves. Teens met at the flagpole and went off to find their friends. Families with beach chairs and blankets filled most of the sandy portion of the beach. Older children ran back and forth to the concession stands, carrying back Cokes and biting into their candy necklaces. Nearby a group of High School football players stood and talked, watching the girls go by, and trying to flex their muscles without being too obvious about it. The grills and picnic tables behind the brick concession stand had been reserved for weeks. One particularly boisterous group was holding a makeshift High School reunion party. It was not Steven's school or his class, but he recognized a basketball buddy so he walked over to say hello.

There were no "Hello, my name is ___" stickers on people's shirts at this party. Most of the people already knew each other or recognized each other quickly. The names change, but the human nature was the same. As at most reunions, some of the guys there had gone gray already or even bald. A few of the girls looked exactly the same, and some showed the signs of early-onset middle aging. The girls chatted in small clusters about current and former relationships, peeking at the boys and gossiping about how they had changed. Groups of guys talked about their High School teams, current pro sports, cars, and the like. Burgers and hot dogs were sizzling on the grill, coolers were being opened and closed, and someone turned up a boom box. WPLJ's Carol Miller introduced "Point of Know Return" by Kansas. Rock music blended in the breeze with laughter, shout-outs, and smoke from the grills.

One of the football players standing near the concession stand walked around the corner and took a long look. He went back to the stand, borrowed a quarter from the girl behind the counter, and called his brother on the payphone. The older brother listened to the summary of who was there and what was going on. It would he hard, if not impossible, to mobilize any response spontaneously, considering the time, distance, and location. The younger brother was asked to keep an eye on the situation, along with three other specific football players. He promised not to do anything before the phone rang again.

Steven left the party and went back to the beach. At the rear of the beach near the parking lot was a pavilion, a shingled roof held up by poles where some families sat in the shade. He stood in line to play the game there. It was a local custom involving tossing a tennis ball on the roof, and the other player had to catch it as it rolled back down off the roof and before it hit the sand, kind of like handball in the City. It was harder than it looked, with limited mobility in the deep sand. He was pretty good at it because his reach was an advantage. As he played, the football players became bored and complacent, and distracted by the bikinis. They reverted to their puffed-up flexing. Steven left the game, jogged into the Sound to cool off, grabbed his towel and left. He had already asked for and received a copy of the attendance figures at the main gate and was halfway to Sound Beach Avenue when the payphone rang at the concession stand. The younger brother looked like someone splashed cold water in his face. One ring. He looked at roofball, but Steven was gone. Two rings. He gave a "What the...?" look at the friends he had trusted. Three rings. He punched one of them in the arm. Four rings. He took a deep breath and answered the phone. The older brother on the other end listened to some ad-libbed lies and was not happy. Frank hung up the phone and stared at the shuffleboard table where a red puck continued its smooth, purposeful path toward its target on the far end of the table.

Chapter Fifteen

Steven called the manager of Putnam Bank & Trust, introduced himself, and asked for a meeting. He explained that he wrote a feature story on the new technology of home banking that was coming out soon and he needed to follow up on a related matter. An hour later he walked into the bank's lobby. The tellers looked up as he passed the main counter. He caught Patty's eye and smiled. She looked terrific, in a new dress from Razooks and jewelry from Betteridge. Without turning her head, she watched him all the way to the manager's office door. The manager sat behind a desk with the bank's logo over one shoulder and a framed lithograph of General Putnam over the other.

"Thank you for seeing me, sir."

"Gladly, have a seat. What's on your mind?"

"I'm working on a theory. If I'm right, it might save this bank a lot of embarrassment, and our town a lot of money. I can't go into the details yet, I have protected sources, but I need a simple favor. I'd like to see a copy of your tellers' work schedule for the last four months. Your job might depend on it." The manager sat dumbstruck, but that last sentence resonated deeply. His job also meant maintaining his mortgage and his family's lifestyle. He nodded and agreed.

"Sure, I can do that. Let me get the master log."

The manager sat across from Steven as he looked at the records. He went through the calendar, isolated Fridays, and jotted down the initials of the employees who worked on the last Friday in May. He put small tally marks next to the initials for each subsequent Friday they worked. When he reached the current week in August, only one teller had worked every Friday all summer. It was nothing the manager didn't already know, but for Steven, it was another step in the right direction.

"Thank you very much, sir. You have been very helpful. I have nothing concrete now, but what I learned can keep me going."

"Is there anything else I can do for you today?"

"Not right now, but I'll certainly be in touch if it gets to a critical point, I promise."

The manager was nervous but relieved at the same time. He walked him out to the front door. Patty heard them clicking across the polished floor but she never looked up.

Steven's next step was a meeting with Chief Graham, who welcomed Steven with a gesture to come in and closed the door to his office. The Chief sat behind a desk with the

Town Seal over one shoulder and a framed photo of himself with the President of the United States over the other.

"Chief, I'm working on a story, an investigation at this point, and I need some help. If I'm right, the Department will bust a huge scam that might be crippling our town."

Chief Graham nodded as if to encourage him to continue.

"If I'm wrong, it's just a reporter trying to be thorough, 'no harm, no foul,' but there's a catch."

"There's always a catch," the Chief said.

"Yes, it has to do with the town's Parks and Recreation Department."

Graham obviously knew the connection, but he never blinked as he kept his focus squarely on Steven.

"I'm not pointing fingers or naming names yet, not without more information, but I think a substantial amount of money...the town's money...is missing. I think it is leaking out of the Parks and Rec. Department."

Graham leaned on his elbow. "Where's this coming from?" the Chief asked.

"Chief, I have my sources."

"Well then, how much money?"

"It's been about ten thousand dollars a week, all summer."

Chief Graham did the math and asked, "How do you know this?"

"I've seen the deposits on bank records of another entity. A similar name to the Greenwich Parks and Recreation Department."

"Who?"

"Chief, I'm sorry, but I can't tell you that, not yet."

"What's the connection?"

"Imagine I had the identity of Ray Grahams, with an 's.' Say I open an account in that name. If I could get my hands on some checks made out to you, the names are so close, especially on handwritten checks, I could probably deposit them. The bogus Grahams gets richer; the real Graham gets poorer."

"Okay, I get that. Move it to this deal."

"Well, I know the impostor's account is growing. I know by how much, and I'm pretty sure I know who owns it. It might be legit. What I *don't* know is if the town's Parks and Rec. account is coming up short, and if so, by how much. If those numbers are close..."

"Yes," Chief Graham interrupted.

Steven pressed forward. "So, could you have a detective meet with the town Auditor and look at the figures for the last four months? If I'm wrong, I apologize in advance. If I'm right, and it's not a crazy coincidence, then it's a major criminal situation, against the town no less, and I will share more information. Of course, we need to maintain the utmost secrecy. Oh, and I have reason to believe speed is essential."

Chief Graham didn't excel and earn awards in Vietnam by making bad decisions. Quick, correct decisions saved lives. He was accustomed to it.

"A major crime against the town? So, what timetable are we looking at?" the Chief asked.

Steven noticed the Chief said "we," then he responded, "The sooner the better, obviously. Can we hit the end of the week, maybe?"

"I think so. Let's try for Friday."

"Yes sir, thank you," Steven said. "Oh, before I go...remember when Sergeant Heaton was promoted and we talked about me doing an article on the Task Force?"

"Ah, yes."

"I've followed up with Heaton's coordinator, and I had a nice conversation with Officers Bittan and Federici a few weeks ago. Looks like it's good to go as soon as I can get into the field."

"That's good. Two fine officers right there. Thank you."

Steven went downstairs. As he was walking out through the heavy steel doors, a detective was already walking into the Chief's office and toward the brown leather chair Steven had just vacated.

A few days later the phone rang on Steven's desk. He put down his coffee, put another call on hold, and answered it.

"Yes, Chief Graham, yes. Thank you for calling...Really? That's close to my numbers too...of course, Chief, of course...I have to get my editor up to speed now, then I'll come see you...thanks, Chief. Bye."

He took a deep breath, locked his fingers together and stretched his hands above his head. He lowered them, exhaled, and pumped his fist.

I'm about to knock the GTC off the front page, he thought, but then he had a stark realization.

Oh my gosh, what about Susie? How would she react if Patty gets busted? Would she care? Would she be mad at me? If I talk to her about it, would she tip off Patty or keep quiet? Should I wait?

And just like that, Steven's professional breakthrough collided with a personal crisis. He had no idea what to do about it.

Chapter Sixteen

The softball season was coming to an end. The YMCA was playing Food Mart at Byram Park, considered by many to be the premier ball field in town. It was the only diamond with lights, so a night game there was a highlight on any team's schedule, and even a day game like this one was special. Behind the infield was a horseshoe of tall rocky cliffs. The field had been cut into the side of a former quarry, one of three quarries there that produced the granite that helped build the two-foot thick walls of the Bruce Park Tavern and several other buildings in Greenwich and in the City, including the Brooklyn Bridge and the Statue of Liberty. The cliffs caused the sounds on the field to echo and also gave the feeling of playing in a stadium. Looking out from home plate, the backdrop included a small beach and boats in Long Island Sound beyond the outfield. It was a picturesque location, for sure.

After Steven was done warming up, he spotted the umpire, Zeke, near the backstop waiting for the game to begin, so he walked over.

"Hey Zeke, how are you?"

"Good Steven, how have you been?"

"Good, good. Look, I'm kind of fascinated by long home runs. It's something of a hobby of mine. What's the longest homer around here you've seen or heard of that stands out?"

"Saw it myself. Dick Stuart hit more than two hundred homers in the Majors. A few years ago he played in a charity fundraiser baseball game behind the old High School."

"Yeah?" Steven interjected.

"Well, he clobbered one to dead center. It cleared the lower parking lot, landed in the *upper* parking lot and bounced against the wing of the building."

"Seriously?"

"You bet."

"That's a big-time homer in a small-time setting."

"Exactly."

"How 'bout this park?"

Zeke pointed to left field. "For instance, look out there, past the light pole, across the parking lot, that little gray maintenance shed. It looks a long way away, right? I'd say it's about three fifty, three sixty, which is like the fence at the bullpen in Shea Stadium."

"Wow, now that you put it that way, that sounds about right. Is it possible to reach the beach behind center field or the boats way out there behind right?" Steven asked.

"You mean on the fly, with a softball?"

"Yeah."

"Is your name Mantle?"

"No," Steven chuckled.

"Well, then keep dreaming, by friend," Zeke said with a laugh.

"I appreciate the lesson."

"Anytime, young fella."

Steven started to leave but he remembered something else and had an idea.

"Oh Zeke, one other thing if you don't mind," Steven said as he stopped and turned back. He decided to ask him if he should tell Susie about his investigation involving Patty, but he didn't have time to lay it all out, so he went for a baseball analogy as a shortcut.

"Yes?"

"What was it like for a Major Leaguer on the bench, when what was best for the team didn't match up with what was best for that player personally? It's kind of a weird feeling, right?"

"No one's asked me that before, but yes, the team comes first. We all probably thought about something bad happening to a starter so we could get a chance to play more, but it's not something we'd never admit or talk about publicly, no way."

"So, you're saying your responsibility to your profession, your life as a pro, has to be held at a higher level than what might be best for you personally?"

"Yeah, I'd say so." Zeke looked at him. "Are you all right?"

"Yeah, I'm gonna be just fine. Thank you."

The YMCA team was having its way with Food Mart, which was missing its usual starting shortstop and leadoff hitter. Once the game was in hand, Steven tried to use his last at bat to see how far he could hit the ball. Popping one into Long Island Sound would be quite an accomplishment, even if it landed in the parking lot then bounced and rolled the rest of the way. Based on his batting practice blast at Bible Street Park, he thought it was possible but highly unlikely. In his last at bat, the variables fell in place once again, as he smashed a towering shot to right-center. The ball seemed destined for wetness, except it squarely struck light pole about three-fourths of the way up and caromed back onto the field. His best chance to add to Zeke's home run list and stroke a once-in-a-lifetime home run ended with the loud clang of leather striking aluminum. A true spectacle had turned into mere speculation instead. He coasted into second, took a look back at the offending light pole, then turned and looked at Zeke behind the plate. Zeke smiled and quickly shook his head "no." Steven grinned back at him, put his hands on his hips, and kicked some dirt off the bag.

Steven's unusual double was quickly forgotten because it was Mark who turned out to be the hero of the game. He hit the game's only true home run, his only one of the season. Most of the outfield had no defined fences, just landscaping between the grass and the parking lot, but there was a legitimate fence and foul pole down the left field line. A stone wall topped by a chain link fence cut across the left field corner. It angled away sharply, and was only reachable if the batter pulled a shot down the foul line over the third baseman's head. The variables fell in place for Mark, as they did for Steven, except Mark's ball cleared the barrier and disappeared into the trees. His face was filled with pride and shock as he realized what happened and downshifted into a home run trot. He was met enthusiastically at home plate by a mob of teammates slapping him on the back and hollering. Steve was right in the middle of it, and Patty jumped off the bench to join in the fun.

She was still their scorekeeper. If she received a score for best sundress, Espadrilles, Ray-Bans and diamond stud earrings, it would have been a runaway victory. After the game, she scurried over to walk with Steven to the parking lot. He slowed a bit to match her stride. It was the first time they had been together since he learned she was Susie's sister, and since he realized she might be siphoning money from the town. *Be careful*, he thought. *Act like nothing's changed.*

"Hey, 'Stretch,' how are you? I saw you at the bank," she said.

"Yes, I'm sorry I couldn't say 'Hi.' I needed a quote from the manager for a technology story. Some Special Report, but it doesn't seem too special to me."

"Oh." She relaxed a bit and continued. "How's the GTC series going?"

"We've pretty much emptied our shelves. We just did the caterers. What's next, the janitors? We're down to the crumbs. Now we're just waiting for the Mayor's announcement Tuesday after Labor Day."

That was more good news for Patty. She had been talking with him all summer at softball games and at the YMCA and thought she knew him well enough by now to get a true read on him. She believed what he said, and was pretty sure that he was not pursuing Greenwich Parking, Reconstruction, and Resurfacing, but she wanted to be more certain. She had no way of getting into his office, so she decided the next best thing was to snoop around his desk at home. Every guy has a desk at home, and she could get into any single guy's home she wanted to, just by arranging a date. She believed it was worth the possibility of spending the night to avoid a last-minute surprise about her phony company and its PO Box in Wilton showing up in the local newspaper. She was ready to try to set it up on her own, but was happy to receive some unexpected help from Mark.

"Hey, the guys say there's a year-end softball party Friday night at The Old Country House. Will I see you there?" Patty asked.

She gave him "The Look." Mark put her up to it. He had seen them talking at every game. The other "Aces" wanted Mark to get Steven to go to the party at The Old Country House. He might not go on his own, just to be with the guys. Mark believed if Patty would be waiting for him, perhaps in one of those sundresses, she would tip the scale. Mark told her it was really important for him and the team for Steven to be at the party. He told her Steven was one of the key players, of course, but a lot of the guys on the team were hoping he could get someone in the Sports Department to write a feature story about them. That would be fun and great publicity for the Y, and maybe even for some of the businesses where they worked. That made sense to her and she was about to agree anyway, then Mark kicked it up a notch. He said because she was so helpful as their scorekeeper, and if she could get Steven to come, the nightclub could make her a VIP guest. They would have a car service for her and some of her friends, with rides both ways, and they would all get Gold Passes for free drinks all night. Backcountry Bobby set that up, and the other "Aces" thought it was a fail-safe plan. It seemed like a sure bet, but the "Four Aces" didn't know what cards Steven held.

Steven caught "The Look" but a warning light flashed in his memory. It triggered a mischievous part of his personality that he cultivated in prep school.

"Friday? Hmm, I think so. That's a great way to wrap it up," he said.

Patty beamed.

"What have you been up to?" he asked.

"Oh, helping with the swim team mostly."

"You got any potential Olympians out there?"

Patty laughed. "No, not a chance. Maybe a college swimmer or two, though."

"When did you start following the Olympics?"

He didn't really need to know, but he felt confident, like he was playing with "house money" at this point.

"A little bit during Mexico City, but I was really young. Then I was more into it in Munich with Mark Spitz. He had all those medals and the mustache. Oh, I liked him a lot."

Steven nodded and went for the follow up. "That was about the time you swept the New Englands, right?"

"Um, yeah."

"Those girls from the Club, I can't remember, who was on that relay team with you?"

His eyes followed the manicured fingernails on her right hand as they went up to scratch her right eyebrow, just like Susie. Patty looked up and thought for a second. He had the real answer he was looking for before she even started talking.

"Let's see, Nancy opened with the backstroke..." She continued, but he zoned out briefly. The three names were not the answer. He had his answer, and she had no idea.

"Oh yes, that was some squad," he said. "Well, I'll see you Friday night then."

She popped up and gave him a little kiss on the cheek. That move, combined with "The Look," never failed her before. Never. She sold it. Mark watched it. As Steven left the park, he was thinking about Patty...not her kiss, the whiff of perfume, or how she brushed against him. Any other man would have definitely been flattered and probably excited, but he felt slightly repulsed. *She's a Trojan horse.* He thought about "The Look." Three images flipped through his memory like a View-Master: Jessica's loving expression, her father's angry stare, and Bill Bowman's astonished reaction to him deciding to leave the

Courant. Steven had learned his lesson about "The Look," and he certainly wasn't going to fall for it now. Then he thought about how Patty abandoned Susie. He felt even more determined to go ahead with his investigation, but he was still unsure about whether to tell Susie about it.

Chapter Seventeen

Steven was sitting in Mike's chair at Putnam Barber Shop but his mind was elsewhere. The clippers created a hum in his ears while his thoughts drifted toward women. No big surprise there; he thought about Susie a lot lately. They were spending more time together and were making that a priority. Often it was his first choice for free time, and he was disappointed when their schedules conflicted. Wendy had been having fun at a weekday summer camp in town, with a great variety of activities including sports, games, swimming, arts and crafts, and occasional field trips. One of her outings was to the Life Savers candy factory in Port Chester. Afterwards she came home all excited with plenty of free samples. She also spent a few weekends with her grandparents in Wilton, which gave Steven and Susan more quality time together, and those particular nights were of a very high quality, no doubt about it.

Then there was Patty—the Queen Guppy turned full-grown dolphin, or perhaps shark. She was the type of girl a younger Steven would often be attracted to but sometimes not be confident enough to approach, leaving her on that fantasy pedestal instead. Their shared background from the summers at the Country Club erased that apprehension, eliminated that "get to know you" stage, and propelled them into their current relationship, whatever that was. Their relationship could not be categorized neatly because he knew things about her family and private life that she didn't know he knew, details that conflicted with and were hidden behind her magazine-cover good looks. Her obvious assets turned heads, like when she and Jennifer arrived at the softball game. Even Jennifer arriving alone might have done that, but the two of them together had an effect more like multiplication rather than mere addition.

Jennifer?

Steven looked up at the photo of Ronny above Angelo's chair.

Ronny's girlfriend, works at Village Travel, Patty's friend.

Mike and Angelo had been chatting in a blend of Italian and English when Steven became more present.

"So Mr. Mike, What's going on? Who's been in?"

Mike ran through the *"Reader's Digest* version" of news, rumors, gossip, names and places. He elaborated only when prompted. Steven made eye contact in the mirror and nodded occasionally. He followed up on a comment about a basketball player from the High School who was riding the bench at the University of Maryland. "ACC ball, that's big time."

"Sure is."

"What about Ronny G; is he still looking for a redhead to complete the *trifecta*?"

Mike stopped cutting and looked up to try to remember. Angelo said something in Italian.

"Oh yes," Mike chuckled. "You and he seem to come in two weeks apart from each other. You know that saying, 'ask him what time it is and he'll tell you how to build a watch?' All I have to do is mention football or girls, and he's off and running."

"Redheads are hard to find. It's not like Ginger from *Gilligan's Island* is walking down the block, right?"

"He said the blonde is much more exciting but way more challenging. And get this...the girls actually know each other."

"Really? How's that happening?"

"He said it's complicated."

"No kidding."

"One of the girls is seeing him on the sly, and somehow orchestrating the whole thing."

"Which one?"

"He didn't say."

Steven knew anyway. Patty introduced Jennifer to him as Ronny's girlfriend. That put the roles in place.

What's Patty's angle? Why would she want to be "the other woman?"

That was interesting to Steven, but not that important. Susie told him she didn't care what Patty was doing; she made that crystal clear. Still, Steven wanted Mike's opinion about it.

"Mr. Mike, I have a problem with two women, too."

"What?!?"

No, nothing like that."

"Oh."

"Seriously, it's more of a family question."

"Okay."

"Family is huge, right?"

"Of course."

"Here we go. I've had someone close to me say she is completely estranged from her sister. They do not get along at all. It's sibling rivalry at its worst. I was told, 'I don't care, never mention that name again.'"

"That's pretty severe."

"Now at the paper I'm doing an investigation, and that sister might be arrested. If I tell my friend, she might think that's big enough to break the silence and tip off her sister, and my work falls apart. If I *don't* tell my friend and her sister gets busted, she might not forgive me because it's such an extreme exception, extreme enough to have ended their standoff. That's a problem because I really care how she feels. So I'm stuck. I might lose a huge story, or I might lose a great woman."

"Wow, I think I've got it. Let me think a minute."

The drone of the air conditioner and the staccato snipping of the scissors were the only sounds in the shop.

"Big Steve, what's the best case scenario? How could this end well?"

Steven looked at the full reflection of the Avenue in the mirror. The door was closed and no one else was there.

"Well, first I take my friend at her word that she's truly on the outs with her sister. I have to trust that. Then, however this investigation turns out, my friend understands I had to comply with the constraints of secrecy in my job, and I also honored the specific wishes to block out her sister. She might be hurt, but she understands it and doesn't hold it against me."

"Big Steve, I would say here like in a lot of situations, look for the best positive outcome and focus your efforts on making that happen."

"That makes sense."

"I know your job is different. It has public responsibilities and obligations that others simply don't. You need to remember that, too."

"Right." Steven looked in the mirror. "Very nice...and the haircut's not bad, either," he joked.

"Thanks, Big Steve."

"I'd say I'd tell you how it turns out, but I'm sure you'll find out anyway."

"Extra, extra, read all about it."

"Thanks."

"Sure thing."

Steven had time for lunch before going back to his office, so he took a flyer that his buddy Chris might be available. He dropped a quarter in a payphone and called him at work. Yes, Chris was available, and Steven caught him just before he headed out the door. They agreed to meet at

Pastrami Dan's, just off the Avenue behind Woolworth's. It was their favorite choice for lunch. He and Chris had been eating there since they were kids, riding bikes downtown on Saturdays to hang out on the Avenue. Pastrami Dan's made some of the best sandwiches in town. They were primarily a carryout business, but they also had a few tables inside for customers who wanted to eat right there. Steven cut through an alley to the restaurant and spotted Chris parking his car. Steven ordered his favorite: roast beef with just enough juice to make it moist without drenching the roll.

Steven and Chris fell into the type of conversation two longtime friends sharing lunch would have: chewing was as important as talking, and neither minded when there was a period of silence. After talking about their softball team, Steven wiped some juice off his chin and switched topics.

"So buddy, I gotta ask you something about my girlfriend, Susie."

"Oh, that waitress at the Diner? How's that going? Getting some free French fries I hope? Is she, ah, taking your order?"

"Ha-ha, very funny. I have a serious question, so try to dial it in for a few minutes. And you have to keep it between us."

"Okay, what'cha got?"

"Susie has a sister she really doesn't get along with. It's a sibling rivalry way beyond cat fight proportions."

"I hear ya," Chris said. Steven knew he had two brothers and a sister.

"Well, they really, really don't get along, to the point that I can't even mention her sister's name around her."

"Okay, so why would you even be talking about her sister anyway?"

"That's the thing, dude. I'm following an investigation at work, and damn if Susie's sister isn't in the middle of it, with a real good chance she could be busted, like for felonies with serious prison time."

"Whoa, so ah, what's the hassle?"

Steven paused to take a slurp of his 7Up.

"Okay, so one scenario is, I keep my mouth shut the sister gets busted and sent to the Big House, and I tell Susie 'Hey, you said not to talk about her,' even though I saw this coming."

"Right, I get that. What else could happen?"

"Well, what if Susie blows her top because I could have told her, and maybe she could have broken through the rivalry and talked some sense into her sister and prevented her from getting caught and getting arrested? Even though they don't get along, how bad do you have to hate your sister to let her go to jail if you have a way to stop it?"

"Well that makes sense too, what's the problem with that?" Chris asked.

"The problem is something called my job, my career. If I tell Susie about this investigation and she blabs to her sister, and she cleans up her act or skips town, then the story is blown to bits and it's all my fault."

"Whoa…so you've got the paper on one side, and Susie on the other?"

"That's right."

"Steve-oh, this is a juggling act, but screwing up your job has got to be way worse than screwing up a relationship."

"Yeah, don't I know it. What are you thinking?"

Chris polished off the last bite of a turkey and cheese sandwich, and wiped the crumbs out of his moustache. "Well, what did you used to do at Country Day when you had to study for a test, but you wanted to talk to a girl on the phone? Of course you studied. School comes first and girls can wait. It's like that now, too. You have to put your work first, and put the girls on the backburner. It's not like she's your wife, man. Do your job the right way. That's the part that's more under your control, so that should be your top priority."

Steven sighed and finished his sandwich. "Yeah, I was thinking the same thing. I just needed to hear someone else say it. Thanks, man."

"No problem. Do you need a hug now?"

"Oh quit it," Steven said, laughing. "So, who are you seeing now?"

"You know me, man. I'm still taking applications for the summer girlfriend position. Got some well-qualified candidates, but no one I want to hire right away. I might need to do follow-up interviews with a few, though."

"What's the better part of that job, the pay or the benefits?"

"The benefits of course? Check it out!" Chris said, laughing.

"Yeah, right! I gotta go back to the office, Thanks for coming over."

"Sure thing. Hey, are you going to the team party at The Old Country House?"

"Yeah, think so. You going?"

"Yeah."

"Okay, I'll see you there," Steven said, pushing away from the table. He balled up the foil and napkins, and lobbed it into a large trashcan in the corner. That gave him spontaneous inspiration.

*****

Steven had the YMCA basketball court pretty much to himself. People usually played Mondays and Wednesdays or Tuesdays and Thursdays. He had always enjoyed shooting baskets by himself…the echoing of the dribbling, the texture of the ball in his hands, the chance to use his imagination, the challenge of refining a repeatable motion. Most players seek a perfect swish, but he liked it better when the ball would clip the inside of the back rim, fire straight through the net seemingly without disturbing it, then maintain its backspin and return to him on three or four bounces. Second best was a swish so pure, the long net would flip up and snag on the rim, requiring him to jump up to release it. That was the most rare basket of all.

It was a type of therapy for him. He enjoyed the rhythm of each shot, the snap of the release, and the momentary feeling of certainty of the ball going in the basket followed a second later by the confirmation. He was lost in the moment, absorbed in the present tense of the task at hand without outside influence or distraction. He had nothing else quite like it, and when it was really good, like on this day, it could bring clarity of thought to unrelated topics in his life. After completing his personal tradition of making three top of the key jumpers in a row before dismissing himself, he went straight home without talking to anyone else or even seeing if Patty was at the pool or if Mark was at the front desk.

Chapter Eighteen

The gravel crunched beneath the tires of Steven's Cutlass as backed into a parking spot near the entrance of The Old Country House and locked up. He wanted to celebrate with the guys, and it would be his last chance for them to be together for several months. Susie understood this, and didn't really want to go to a big, smoky club after working on her feet all day. Steven was relieved because he knew Patty would be there and he didn't want to get caught up in that triangle, and he had told Susie he would visit her at the Diner the next morning. Their team's third-place finish out of sixteen teams was the YMCA's best season in several years. With Richard's Men's Clothing Store winning back-to-back titles, everyone else was playing for second place, anyway. He spotted Chris and went over.

"Hey man, what's up?" Steven said.

"Long time no see, Steve-oh," he joked.

"How's it going tonight?"

"Cool, cool."

"Who's here?"

"Just about the whole team. Mark of course, I've seen most of the fellas already."

"Anyone else we know?"

"Well...oh, I saw Patty. She's here somewhere."

"Okay."

Chris introduced a couple of girls he graduated with from St. Mary's. They all spent a few minutes talking about mutual friends who went to St. Mary's after Greenwich Country Day. The girls' ring-free left hands gripped Budweiser bottles wrapped in napkins.

"I'll get one of those, too. Anyone need anything?" Steven asked.

He shouldered his way over to the bar and made eye contact with the bartender and clearly enunciated "Bud." He took a look around as he waited. He could look over the top of the crowd and see most of the people there. The dance floor was hopping with couples and small groups of girls. Amii Stewart's "Knock on Wood" thumped out of massive Marshall speakers in every corner. The DJ was in an elevated booth. He stroked his mustache as he flipped through a crate of records. Steven noted signs for "Bathrooms" and "Emergency Exit," a lit walkway going to the other part of the club, and a small, plain door with the nameplate "Manager" near the DJ's booth. The bartender shouted, "Bud." Steven snapped around and paid.

Over the next hour or so he visited with a few of the other guys from the team. Mark seemed a bit preoccupied, but Steven figured it was because he was holding court as a regular in his favorite bar. He hadn't seen Patty though, not yet. Eventually he worked his way back with Chris and the girls, who were talking to some other friends.

Even though the fallout from the "The Scandal" had subsided, and it had been a long time since he received any threats, Steven still had his radar up for suspicious activity in public. It didn't matter whether he was at the library, the grocery store, or the Dairy Queen, by acquired habit, he'd scan faces and notice where the exits were. He was aware that he was doing this even in obscure places, like sitting in Mike's chair getting his hair cut, but it was second nature to him now.

He was enjoying the night until he noticed there were more big football-type guys there then he would usually see in such a gathering. They could have been Security, but they were all wearing different shirts, not like the black and silver "The Old Country House" polo the bouncer at the front door was wearing. He recognized at least a couple of them from that night at the Indian Harbor Inn earlier that summer. A bloated sunburned man stood under the "Emergency Exit" sign, as he did at the Inn. Steven saw a couple of them glance at him then dart their eyes away to look at each other. Mark was leaning against

184

the wall near the Manager's door next to the DJ booth. He seemed to be part of the visual Ping-Pong.

"Chris, I'm gonna check out the other side. Be back in a bit."

"Okay, man."

Steven went around the dance floor and down the lit hallway that connected the two rooms of the club. As he did, Patty and a group of her friends were coming the other way. They looked like a casting call for *Charlie's Angels*.

Oh, here we go.

"Weeeeell, 'Stretchy Stretch,' I'm so glad you is here," she said. He could see the reflection of the colored disco lights in her glassy eyes. Patty held a drink in her left hand and put her right hand against the wall to regain her balance.

"You got some 'Guppies' here, Patty?"

"Nooo, these some my college frienss. Hey, let me talks to him for a minutes," she slurred. Patty's friends shrugged and walked into the main room, each of them carrying a drink and wearing a gold paper band around their wrists. Patty had one also. She smiled the uninhibited smile of someone who had been enjoying an open bar, and as though she was already celebrating something she had not won yet. Because he was sober and she clearly was not, he was confident that would give him the upper hand here, no matter what they talked about.

Steven stepped to the other side of the hallway to let another couple through. He scooted around Patty so the main dance floor was behind her. He half-sat and leaned against a hand railing, which lowered him closer to her height and made it easier to hear her. It wasn't as loud in the hallway as it was in either room, so they didn't need to shout to be heard. She moved half a step closer to him, switched her drink to her other hand and grabbed his arm briefly before repositioning it on the rail.

"You having fun?" he asked.

"Yeah, we've been here since ah, for a while."

"Me too. I guess I didn't see you sooner because it's so crowded."

"Well, you see me now, right?"

She did a half-spin to show off her new dress, but wobbled a bit on her heels, as if even that small movement made her dizzy. The lights bounced off her diamond earrings. She was overconfident about her Park Plan being safe. Unfortunately for Patty, her overconfidence and inebriation was a bad combination. What Backcountry Bobby liked to say held true—"Hang around some liquored-up people who are still coherent, and it's amazing what they will say and what you can learn."

"That's a pretty dress. You look like a million bucks," he said, amused at the appropriateness of the cliché. It flew right over her hair-sprayed head.

"You like? I got it for Labor Day, but I couldn't wait. I'm sooo excited. Jennifer booked me a trip in Bahamas. I haven't been there years ago and I wanna go back as an, a adult. Gonna be blastin'!"

"Yeah, for sure," he said. He was thinking about what Susie said was a family joke. *When I win the lottery, I'm moving to the Bahamas.*

Some lottery, he thought.

"When are you leaving? Do you need a ride?" he asked. He cared about only one of those answers.

"Nooo, I'm fines. Friday after works."

"Wow, have a great time."

"I wanna have a great time…now," she said, remembering her plan to get into his house. That was why she was there that night. The VIP package was icing on the cake, but her unexpected alcohol-induced haze made it tougher for her to focus on her primary goal. She tried a drunken version of "The Look" but it was ineffective, so she slid closer to him instead. He could smell a pungent mixture of perfume, sweat, and alcohol.

"Let's celebrate the softball. Whaddya say we gets outta heres?" she said.

She slowly shifted her weight side to side in rhythm to the music as she struggled to fix her gaze on him.

"Where do you feel like going?" he asked.

Patty was slightly confused. Usually when she said, "Let's get out of here," men burned rubber like "Big Daddy" Don Garlits's dragster, much less asked more questions. She scratched her right eyebrow for a second.

"Weeell, it's like boiling in heres. I wanna cool off, maybe go swimming. Heeey, you gotta pool, don'tchas?" She knew full well that he did. "You haven't seen me sweeem in like forevers. Les go skinny dipping," she said.

He smiled at her, and she incorrectly assumed why he was smiling. Actually, he was merely amused she was so drunk. He stood up and looked past her into the main room and dance floor. The DJ was between songs so the lighting was consistent there for the time being. Mark was one step up on the DJ booth, looking right toward them. He had moved up a step when Steven sat on the railing. A bit to Mark's right, a burly guy in a tight shirt and a flat-top turned his head away from them, nodded at something Mark was saying, and gestured toward the bloated, sunburned man who was still standing beneath the Emergency Exit sign. Steven's mind kicked up a notch.

No way…Patty's part of their crew! All that happy chitchat all summer, they were setting me up! This is a trap! Think Steven…

"Yeah, you're right, it's getting hot in here," he said, looking at his watch. He felt like he had to hurry. He knew about Bingo from the guys on the team, which meant one o'clock might be a very bad time to still be in The Old Country House.

"Did you drive up here?"

"Nooo, I came wiff friends."

"Okay, Sweetie. It's a quarter to one now. You find your friends, tell them you're leaving with me, and I'll meet you out front at one o'clock, okay?"

"Sure, 'Stretchy,' whatchu says."

Patty turned and caught her balance again. She tugged her dress down with her free hand and walked toward the main dance floor. He admired the view then shook his head once, sighed, and snapped out of it.

The "Four Aces" were using their Bingo Night plan that night, too. They expected to have their delegates fully staffed and in position by one, and either have Patty slap him in the face so they could pick a fight with Steven or jump him in the parking later whenever he left or at closing time. That was up to Bobby, Mark, and Alex, who were inside. Frank was dozing in a car outside because of his restraining order, and the "Aces" didn't want Steven to see him.

Steven followed Patty to the dance floor and cut over to where Chris was camped out.

"Dude, I need a huge favor," Steven said.

"Cool, Steve-oh, what is it?"

"This sounds crazy, but trust me. Go on the dance floor and in about two minutes, pretend you blew out your knee and hit the deck, yelling, screaming and swearing."

"Say what?!?"

"For real, cause a big scene then shake it off and hobble out. Here's forty bucks."

Steven turned his back to where Mark was standing, and casually slid two twenties under Chris's beer bottle on the table.

"I'll explain it to you later, I promise."

Chris looked up at him and could tell he was dead serious. He took one deep chug to finish his beer, picked the money up, and put the bottle down.

"Okay, I'll do it."

"I owe you big time."

Steven walked around the dance floor and toward the bathrooms. He felt several pairs of eyes following him. Chris took the hand of one of his St. Mary's friends and blended into the crowd. The bathrooms were down a short hallway from the main dance floor. A line of women hugged one wall, and Steven stood behind two guys waiting on the other side. From a few steps down the hallway, the view of the main room was severely limited, like a racehorse wearing blinders. The reverse-angle meant only a small portion of the people in the main room could see into the hallway and from his lofty perspective he could see who was looking that way and who was not. He figured his adversaries would be looking for his head above the crowd as he walked out of the hallway in a couple of minutes. Just as the men's bathroom door opened and closed, Chris shrieked in pain and fell to the floor, clutching his knee in apparent agony. He wailed and screamed, pounded his fist against the floor, and let loose a string of expletives that belied his Catholic upbringing. The woman he was dancing with bought it totally. She yelled for help and looked around with a panicked expression. Most of the people who were dancing stopped or slowed down and stared at Chris. The bouncer at the front door told the people waiting in line "wait here" as he left his stool and pushed his way onto the floor to see what was going on. Even the bartenders stopped pouring drinks. Chris had the attention of nearly everyone there.

That was just what Steven was hoping for. He headed out of the short hallway, but in a low-crouching duck-walk, like Groucho Marx, along an interior wall and toward the front door. He continued to bend down so his head didn't

191

hover over the crowd like a lighthouse. Those big dudes he was concerned about were distracted by Chris's injury, and otherwise never saw his head bobbing above the crowd. As Steven approached the front door, he stood all the way up and stepped into the parking lot, digging for his keys.

Patty was *not* outside and that didn't slow him down one bit.

The bouncer saw a flash of motion and light near his vacated sentry spot as Steven briefly filled the doorframe. "Hey, there he goes!"

The shout from the bouncer caught the attention of the "Four Aces'" beef brigade, but the blaring music slowed their communication. They fought their way through the crowd and stormed out the door. Steven was already in his Cutlass and two turns through rows of cars. He looked out the window and saw taillights fire up and the interior lights flash on when three doors flew open on a big vehicle with two more doors on the back end. *Four doors, maybe five guys. A big old Chevy Suburban. It has to back out and turn through those tight rows of parked cars,* he thought.

Steven approached the end of the parking lot and wanted to turn left on North Street, toward Greenwich. He gunned it to hop in front of a Volkswagen Beetle headed in the same direction. He snapped off his car stereo, a Beatles song, ironically, so he could concentrate better. One last look over his shoulder and the Suburban was fishtailing through the gravel. *Create space and go over the defense, just like basketball,* he thought. He had a head start and the Beetle was slowing down his pursuers. If and when the Suburban swerved out to pass the Beetle, he would probably see it. He was focused on the Suburban. If there was another car coming, it would be following the Suburban, rather than actively chasing him. The Suburban held his primary pursuers.

Back in The Old Country House, Patty was checking her makeup in the chrome of a beer sign and was trying to remember why she was about to walk out the door. She gave up and went to find her friends. Mark came out of the Manager's office. He had dipped in there for just a couple of minutes, but it was the wrong couple of minutes. He hadn't heard all the commotion because of the soundproofed door and the loud music. All of his boys were gone…and Steven too. He did the only thing he could think of that made sense. Seeing they were not in the parking lot either, he went back home and waited for the phone to ring.

The Cutlass zipped south on North Street. In his rearview mirror he saw four headlights side by side, meaning the Suburban was passing the Beetle. *If they're even, I'm leavin',* Steven thought.

He drove a bit faster through the darkness on the edge of town. The speeding Suburban was a menacing vehicle, to say nothing of the Neanderthals piled into it. A huge, heavy, high-center-of-gravity vehicle to begin with, it was now more than one thousand pounds heavier. It wouldn't handle well. The driver would have to be careful in the turns then try to catch up on the straight-aways of this two-lane road. Steven knew his Cutlass had an advantage. It was no Corvette or even a Mustang, but it was better than the Suburban.

He could have taken his chances weaving through tangent residential roads, but he had another idea, a much better idea. He had information the Suburban's driver couldn't possibly know, and he had about three minutes to get to where he wanted to be. The Merritt Parkway was coming up. It was an older roadway, and one of its distinguishing features was very short, sharply curved ramps. They were nothing like the long, easy-merging runways on the Interstates. These ramps were tight and abrupt. He floored it down North Street to create more space, losing sight of his pursuers.

Stone walls that originally marked the borders of farms blurred by on both sides, in some spots quite close to the road. At his speed, if a car pulled out of a driveway in front of him, he wouldn't have enough time to react. It was a calculated risk that the residents along upper North Street had no reason to leave their plush estates in the wee hours of the morning. With his high beams on and no oncoming traffic, he took liberties with the double yellow line, straightening out some of the curves and staying farther away from those walls. He had done all he could when he reached the most dangerous part of the road. North Street dipped noticeably and banked sharply to the left, like a roller-coaster ride. The moon reflected beautifully off a lake to his left, but he had no time to enjoy the view, much less take his eyes off the road. That same moon reflected angrily off a rusty guardrail hugging the right side of the road, just inches from his car.

Steven approached the ramp to the Parkway, slammed on his brakes, skidded, and turned a sharp right. The tires chattered as the Oldsmobile strained to stay on four wheels. The Cutlass leveled out, and he was relieved there was no traffic in that spot on the Parkway. He drifted off the ramp, merged via centrifugal force, and sped away.

The Suburban's driver never saw the Cutlass turn and flew by the Parkway, intent on catching up. The Suburban bounced over the Parkway's overpass, briefly rising on its shocks and almost coming off the ground. The driver regained control around a shallow left turn approaching the other half of the North Street exit, only to be surprised to see what Steven already knew was there…a police DWI checkpoint. The driver's first reaction, besides swearing, was to swerve across the road, believing there was more room there, but not much on this two-lane road. The driver stood on his brakes. Thinking he was going to veer off the road, he turned the wheel back to the right, but just a bit too much. The Suburban tipped over and skidded in a shower of sparks.

Police officers dove for cover off the road as the Suburban slid toward them and smashed into one of the police cruisers set up to funnel traffic. The impact sent the Suburban spinning off the side of the road to the left, and the police car spinning off the side of the road to the right, like shuffleboard pucks caroming into the game's gutters at Bruce Park Tavern. Another police cruiser was untouched. Officer Federici raced to his dashboard and called for emergency help.

"F-one-five calling base," he said.

"Go ahead, F-one-five," the dispatcher said.

"I've got a ten-fifty, possibly eight victims, need a ten-fifty-one, ten-fifty-two, ten-fifty-three."

"What's your twenty?"

"DWI checkpoint, North Street at the Merritt."

"Ten-four."

"F-one-five, out."

The night editor at the *Greenwich Time* office heard the same conversation on his scanner. He checked the codes on an emergency signals list, reached for the phone and immediately sent a reporter to the hospital, and a reporter and photographer to the scene. He also called the supervisors in Layout and Printing to determine how much could be changed before their deadlines.

Officer Bittan scrambled back onto his feet and sprinted to the mangled Suburban. It was on its side and wrapped around an oak tree with its roof crushed. The driver was the only person wearing a seat belt. Three passengers were killed instantly, and three people would be rushed to Greenwich Hospital with critical injuries.

When Mark heard what happened, he stayed in a dark room by himself for a day and a half. When he came out, he did nothing but drive directly to and from the YMCA every day for a month, never exceeding the speed limit. He even stopped drinking, as he had promised himself so many times before. This "Ace" became a low card, not a high card.

Chapter Nineteen

Susie had already seen the headline and photo in the paper before Steven walked into the Diner the next morning. He plopped down into his usual booth and subconsciously scanned the room to see who else was there. Susie came right over with a cup of coffee. She was anxious to launch into a big conversation, but she was aware that she was at work and in a public place.

"Hey, how are you? Are you all right? Did you see that accident? Was it before or after you came home? I was worried. What do you think..."

"Susie, Soos, I'm okay, I'm okay," he calmly interrupted. He already had time to process what happened and his role in (or at least a connection to) the accident. It was scary for sure, but he tried to isolate and compartmentalize it as a news story only, especially now in front of Susie. He briefly touched her hand as she was put the coffee cup down on the table. She looked quickly over her shoulder at the kitchen then turned back to him. It was not too busy, but she grabbed her notepad as if to take an order. Steven held a menu in one hand as they talked in hushed tones.

"I tried to call you from the kitchen, but there was no answer."

"I was probably in the shower or already out the door. I just found out about it this morning, too. I didn't see that crash."

"The paper didn't have many details. A truck slammed into a police car? What happened?"

"It's hard to say but three people are dead and three are in the hospital. Police are still sorting it out. I didn't recognize any of the names I've heard, except for one of the people in the hospital… Frank Castino."

"Who?"

"Frank Castino, the owner of Bruce Park Tavern. Remember, *that* Frank Castino?"

"Ohhh."

"He's alive but all banged up. Our sources say he was the driver, but the police have not confirmed that yet."

"That's crazy. Did you see him up there?"

"No, I did see a bunch of my softball friends, though," Steven said, changing the topic slightly. "It was kinda funny, seeing my softball friends when they've had some beers letting loose on the dance floor, it's like some *Saturday Night Fever* wannabes out there."

"That's funny."

"Yeah. Oh, and I gotta tell ya, your sister was there, too."

Susie lowered her notebook and put her hand on her hip. She narrowed her eyes and waited for him to continue.

"I guess she was there because it was the softball party, but she was cruising around with a big group of her girlfriends."

"Steven, I thought we went over this," Susie said, looking around the room again to see if anyone was listening. "I couldn't care less about her and what she's doing. We're done. I've already moved on. I would appreciate it if you do not bring up her name, and I certainly don't need any updates about what she's doing. If she can't find any time for her big sister and her only niece, my daughter…" Susie paused but quickly continued. "Please, just drop it. There is nothing in the world that she could be doing that I'd care about. Not a thing, Trust me. It's something I can't keep fighting. Trust me."

"What if she was in some sort of big trouble?"

"Not…a…thing."

Susie folded her arms and look out the window toward the Y and the bank. Her eyes started to well up just slightly, but she blinked hard to stop it. Steven wanted to give her a hug, but it was not appropriate there.

"Hey, hey, it's okay," he said quietly. "I understand now. I'm all about my Miss Baker, remember?"

"Yes, I know," she said, looking down a bit.

"I won't bring up her name ever again, I promise." he said.

"Thank you."

They looked at each other so deeply it was like their whole souls merged.

Chapter Twenty

The "Life in the Next Decade" Special Report ran in the middle of August then the last batch of profiles and sidebars ran for a week leading up to the GTC announcement. Mayor Bentley's big press conference with the details and contracts was set for Tuesday for the Labor Day tie-in. Steven was squared away with his assignments.

Meanwhile, he had huddled a few times with his senior editor and Chief Graham to discuss the Putnam Bank & Trust investigation. They all agreed the information was convincing, even if somewhat circumstantial. The Chief said there was enough meat on the bone for the police to justify using a "probable cause" search warrant to see the records of the travel agency where Jennifer worked, without her knowledge. Police confirmed Patty was leaving the country on a Friday night flight from New York City to Nassau. The senior editor backed Steven in protecting his sources. Chief Graham believed it was worth the effort. The newspaper, the Police Department, and the town were all in this together now.

The banker who supplied Steven's information agreed to participate if his name and his company would remain anonymous so he wouldn't get in trouble with his bosses. He would take the express train back from the City to meet them in his Greenwich office on Friday afternoon, on the cusp of the Labor Day weekend.

A plain-clothes policeman walked through the Putnam Bank & Trust branch Friday after lunch. He had been given Patty's description. She was there and easy to identify. Steven drummed a pencil at his desk and looked out the ground-level window at the employee parking lot and a dumpster in the alley behind the Avenue. He watched the clock's hands crawl before he stood up and poked his head into his editor's office.

"I'm going," he said.

Steven and Sgt. Sanderson arrived at the banker's office just minutes apart. Everyone else had already cleared out to start the weekend. Their small talk with the banker was tense, given the circumstances. The banker gave the Sergeant a brief overview about the printer and what to expect. He ran a demonstration so the Sergeant would be familiar with what to look for. It was a streamlined version of what Steven had learned from him weeks earlier.

In the last hour before the bank's closing time, Patty was trying to maintain a sense of normalcy, but her mind was racing. She had stopped transferring money a couple of weeks earlier. She became nervous after Steven visited the manager and she didn't want to press her luck. She didn't remember much about that night at The Old Country House, and nothing at all between seeing Steven in the hall and waking up alone in her own bed. Besides, she used the time to focus her attention on the essential task of using a link to navigate from the Parks & Recreation Department's account directly into the town's primary account.

She found out about it while working on a special assignment. The bank's computer was connected to an IBM "System/370," which guided funds from account to account, like a police officer directing traffic in an intersection on the Avenue. It didn't take her long to figure out how the Parks & Recreation account and the town's other accounts fed through it like rivers pouring into the ocean. She liked the ocean, and the islands in it. Her bank's access, a gap in security, and the password "Israel Putnam" opened the town's ocean-like account, expanding her horizon. That allowed her to see how funds moved between the town and its departments. In particular, she studied the accounts and had a pretty good idea what the perceived ceiling was for a large transaction, but not so large that it would draw extraordinary attention. She decided on a big, round number that would go through easily but also might look like an accounting error. She had thought all along this was the perfect time to go for it. The bank would be closed for the three-day weekend then it was another month until the Town's new fiscal year kicked in. It was her personal lottery. She retraced her preparations. Her small-scale tests had worked. Now, like the champion swimmer she used to be, she waited for the starter's gun.

The Sergeant subconsciously tapped his gun as he sat in the banker's office. Only occasional static interruptions from his radio cut into the silence. Then, the computer made three distinctive clicks and the printing module rotated, whirred, and aligned on the left edge. It was five minutes before the top of the hour, before the bank's closing time, before a three-day holiday weekend. The previous printout Steven saw showed deposits of around ten thousand dollars each week, with more than twenty thousand dollars before Memorial Day and close to fifty thousand dollars before the Fourth of July. The new printout started feeding. The printing module worked in both directions line by line. The banker lifted the front corner so they could all read it as it came through.

"Okay, here it comes," the banker said.

"There's the twenty-one thousand and change at Memorial Day," Steven narrated. "Now here's June...nine thousand, nine, eleven...here comes Fourth of July weekend, yep, forty-eight thousand plus. Now smaller again through August. C'mon Patty, what's it gonna be for Labor Day?"

Steven answered his own question. "Probably doubling the spike again, this time a hundred thou."

The three men leaned in closer as the printer paused.

"There it is. Fifty...no, what? Five, what?" Steven asked.

The banker adjusted his grip on the corner of the page. They all saw it, but no one could believe it. The woman with the legendary figure had chosen an equally remarkable financial figure.

"Five million dollars," the banker announced.

"Oh…" was all Steven could say.

The three men had the same eyebrow-raising reaction, but all muted by various professional protocols. Just seconds after they digested that entry, the computer spat out another one, draining the entire account and depositing it into a bank in the Bahamas.

"We're good," the Sergeant said.

"Okay," the banker said.

The Sergeant stepped to the side and radioed a private frequency. "It's confirmed," he said.

The banker carefully tore off the printout and placed it in a copy machine. He kept one copy, gave Steven one, and gave the Sergeant one, plus the original. After quick and earnest handshakes and goodbyes, they all left.

Patty dropped some papers into her Louis Vuitton handbag, closed up as usual, and breezed out the front door. Her happy face then dissolved into a more concentrated look. She walked across the street to the YMCA. Police in hidden surveillance locations in the office building across Mason Street and in storefronts on the other side of the Post Road radioed headquarters with that information. She had an important piece of luggage in her locker, and more in her car. She walked briskly through the familiar halls to the locker room. She spun the Master

Lock and removed a red nylon YMCA gym bag. She dropped the lock into the bag and started to leave. As she passed the pool, a young girl and her mother came through the door. The girl started talking a-mile-a-minute, telling Patty about her latest swim meet and thanking her for the instructions that helped her lower her time for a second-place finish. Patty listened and smiled nervously, balancing between being polite and trying to leave. After an agonizing delay that was actually less than a minute, she excused herself and continued toward the lobby.

What Patty didn't know was while she was in the Y, Sgt. Sanderson had radioed Chief Graham and the dispatcher had relayed the go-ahead for all the officers hiding outside to converge on the scene. She was just approaching the lobby when she saw flashing lights through a window. Police cruisers came squealing up the Post Road, simultaneously parking and blocking traffic right outside the window. She started to sweat and briefly tried to figure out how this could have happened so quickly, let alone who knew, but she had no quick or easy answer. She had several questions but right then they would have to wait. She had to get out of there and get to her car.

She turned and went back down the hallway past the pool, walking as fast as she could—not trotting, jogging, or running. She felt she still had a degree of control. She made two turns, went past the entrances of both locker rooms, then through a door and down another hallway toward the rear exit. As she approached that door, she looked through the square glass-and-crossed-wires window and spotted two police cruisers blocking the mouth of the rear parking lot. Her mouth went dry. This was no longer a time for walking, not even a fast walk.

Patty turned back and hurried down the hallway, through the door, then away from the locker rooms. She maneuvered through the ancient, maze-like building until she found another door marked "stairs." It was not the main stairwell, but the back stairwell. She pushed through the heavy, creaky door, entered the musty, dingy cement foyer, hesitated for a moment then hustled up to the second floor, which had mostly offices and meeting rooms. She had not spent much time up there, but the hallways had a similar pattern to some of the first floor. She needed a place to sit, hide, and figure out how to get to her car. Most of the doors were locked. She pulled on handles until she found one that was open. She took a peek inside, deemed it suitable, slipped into the room, and locked the door behind her.

While Patty ran up the back stairs, policemen entered through the front door. Mark looked up from a clipboard at the front desk. He had seen police in the Y many times before, but this time was different. He could tell right away by their body language that something was brewing, so he stood up and waited patiently.

The lead officer was talking on his walkie-talkie as other officers poured in behind him. "Back entrance secure? Ten-four."

Mark could feel their sense of urgency. He knew typical warrants didn't have this many officers or this much energy. As the Building Supervisor, it was his building at the moment.

"This could be a big deal," Mark muttered to himself then he spoke up. "I'm Mark Langford, Building Supervisor. How can I help?"

"Officer Kingsley. We observed a woman enter this building and we believe she is still here. We need to find her. Patricia Callahan."

Mark had no idea what Patty could have done to draw such attention.

"Well, yeah, Patty's a lifeguard here, but she works nights, so I haven't seen her today," he said honestly.

More officers came through the door. Kingsley said, "We need your help here. Tell us about the building."

"Okay. There are four floors. A basement, this one, two upstairs, plus two stairwells." He quickly described the layout. He could feel the situation developing into some sort of opportunity. Kingsley huddled briefly with the other officers. Two would stay in the lobby and other pairs went to each floor. Mark helped the officers go in the right direction then he paired up with Kingsley.

"Let's start with the women's locker room," Kingsley commanded.

"Sure."

Mark led the officer through a door, down a hall, and into the pool area. They walked directly to the lifeguard on duty. After a brief conversation, she blew an air-horn, clearing the pool of the four adults swimming laps. The swimmers exchanged confused looks as they reached for their towels. The lifeguard went into the locker room to make sure anyone inside was dressed. She came back out and told Kingsley, "It looks empty, go ahead."

Kingsley and Mark went inside. They pulled back shower curtains, looked into bathroom stalls, and opened closets. The lockers were too small for adults to hide in and there was not much else to see. Kingsley radioed the officers assigned to the ground floor with an update. They went back to the pool, waved to the lifeguard, and headed back to the lobby.

The two officers sent to the basement were already in the lobby. The basement was locked and not accessible to the public as usual so they found nothing significant there, and the back stairwell was clear. The two officers assigned to the third floor, the men's dormitory, came down the stairs. Everyone they asked said they had not seen any women up there all day, much less somebody looking like Patty. The officers who finished the main floor sweep came back through another door. The gym, the weight room, the men's locker room, the main offices and the bathrooms were all clear. Finally, the two officers from the second floor showed up.

"We had some trouble up there," one officer said.

"How so?" Kingsley asked.

"Most of the doors were locked, so we can't be certain the floor is clear."

"I've got the keys," Mark offered.

"Let's go," Kingsley said.

Mark gave the three officers a preview as they went up the stairs while the others fanned out across the lobby. "Well, we have some meeting rooms and some offices. We keep all those locked unless they're being used, so count'em out." Mark said.

"What's left over?" Kingsley asked.

"Bathrooms," Mark said.

"Clear," one officer said.

"And a few others that can be locked from the inside doorknobs," Mark said. "The first one is on the right. It's a janitorial closet. A string hangs down for the light."

Mark fingered his key chain as he approached the door. He isolated the correct key and let an officer open it. The other officers tensed slightly as they stood in support positions. The officer opened the door and pulled a cord to turn on an overhead light, but no one was in there.

"Okay, now this one has office supplies. It's tiny, no lights," Mark said.

He found that key and again let the police open the door, but it was empty, too.

"The only other room is right over there. It's a storage room for pool equipment. The light switch is inside on the right, chest high. It's weird, though...there's no floor, just a walkway around the edge and catwalks that go back and forth, so be careful."

He chose not to elaborate about the ceiling tiles beneath the catwalks. He produced the "P4" key with a flourish, and handed it to one of the officers. He turned the "P4" key, removed it, and handed the key chain back to Mark. He opened the door and reached inside for the lights. The officer walked inside, going straight along the perimeter walkway. Another officer entered and turned right, effectively going in the opposite direction around the rectangular area and past a stack of kickboards. Mark took a peek inside and noticed one of the ceiling tiles had been lifted open. He glided across a catwalk for a closer look, and saw a pair of high heels on the locker room floor.

"She jumped!" Mark shouted. "She's in the women's locker room on the main floor. Go!"

Kingsley immediately radioed the officers in the lobby, sending them in the right direction. The upstairs officers were already out of the storage room and flying down the hall as Kingsley was finishing his call. Mark looked at

Kingsley for direction then started jogging behind the sprinting officers. By the time Mark and Kingsley were back downstairs and between the lobby and the pool, Patty had been apprehended. She had left the locker room, saw the police and doubled back into it. She had been caught underneath the missing ceiling tile, which sat askew inside the pool storage room that could be opened with a key marked "P4."

Now in handcuffs, Patty was escorted past Mark and out the front door of the YMCA. She was tan and squinting in the late afternoon sun. She looked toward the bank around the corner on Mason Street, where her car was parked. She made it only three steps down the wide, granite stairway before she heard Chief Graham on the sidewalk below.

"Patricia Callahan, you are under arrest."

Patty's nose scrunched up. Chief Graham read her the Miranda Rights, right there on the front steps. Her disbelief dissolved into tears. Another officer opened her gym bag, revealing wrapped stacks of cash. A plane ticket was in her purse. Inside the Y, Mark cupped his hands against a window to better see what was going on. Steven hopped out of a parked car and started taking notes. A second reporter ran over from a parking lot across from the bank. A photographer stepped out of another car and began taking pictures. His photo of Chief Graham with one hand on Patty's head guiding her into the back seat of a police car would fill the front page above the fold the next day.

Everyone within a block heard the sirens and the commotion. Customers at the Diner left their tables and came outside to watch. Susie stood firmly on the top step and stared unwaveringly at her sister in the back seat of the police car until it left to go back to headquarters. As the police left, so did the onlookers. Steven knew he could catch up with Chief Graham and he had to interview Mark, but he would still be in the Y for the rest of the day. He huddled quickly with the other reporter and photographer, thanked them and excused himself.

Steven walked down the steps from the YMCA and went toward the Diner as he had done so many times before. He stood on the curb waiting for the traffic light to change. He looked over his shoulder at bank, where police were now inspecting a silver Datsun 280Z with Connecticut plates 200IM in the parking lot. The other reporter and photographer were waiting in the shade of the bank's blue glass façade and watching to see what might develop. Steven looked both ways and walked across the street. With the exception of a brief minute when Susie went back inside to tell the manager she was taking her break, she had been perched on that step. He knew she was there and had been waiting for him. In the course of the several strides it would take to cross the Post Road and go to the Diner, he'd have to figure out what to say, and some of that would depend on what *she* said. He preferred planned rather than spontaneous, but this was a most unusual and potentially combustible situation.

He walked up the sidewalk to the Diner, where Susie had been standing for several minutes. He stopped when he was about three feet away. He looked at her, looked at his reporter's notebook, and dropped it in the grass next to him. They both watched the notebook spiral down to the ground, its pages fluttering as it fell. He looked at that notebook on the ground for a second before turning his head up at her. Susie reached into her apron, took her own notepad, and tossed it down on top of his, then smiled that Susie smile.

"Hello, Mr. Rollins."

"Why Miss Baker, so good to see you again."

Steven took half a step forward so they were now less than an arm's length apart. Susie came down one step, so they were now at eye level.

"Good move," he said. "Where you'd learn that?"

"A very, *very* close friend taught me well."

"Hmmm."

Susie waited for him to continue.

"Are you okay?"

"Yes, that was a little bizarre, like I was watching a movie instead of real life, but I'm fine."

"I was gonna tell you, but you made it so obvious…"

"You're right," She interrupted. "I made that really clear. And maybe it's better I *didn't* know. That would have been even more bizarre. But you were already here, so when did *you* know?"

Steven sighed. "Well, it takes a while for water to boil, you know. It's a long story, and I'm still writing it," he said with a smile. "Actually, I have more interviews to do. I'd love to tell you all about it, but not here, not now. You deserve better."

"You *are* my better," she said.

He closed the distance and gave her a big hug. His long arms wrapped all the way around her. Her body heaved once like she was about to cry, but she didn't.

"This will all be over soon, and no matter how it ends, Soos, I'll be around," he whispered in her ear.

She stifled a sniffle and whispered back, "I know you will."

Chapter Twenty-one

Forty miles away in Wilton on that Friday afternoon, police investigators opened PO Box 222, assigned to Greenwich Parking, Reconstruction and Resurfacing.

Four days later, Mayor Bentley was still fielding questions about the "Callahan Case," even at his much- ballyhooed Tuesday morning press conference to release the details about the Greenwich Transportation Center. Patty's arrest had turned a slow holiday weekend into a full breaking news situation. Steven, of course, was right in the middle of the coverage. The *Greenwich Time* hit the nail on the head with its GTC previews. Steven was riding two massive waves at once: the biggest town improvement project in ten years, and the biggest embezzlement case in the state's history. The New York City newspapers had to play catch-up, not only in the reporting, but also doing their own localized angle with their banks, versions of "Could it happen here?" Even the New York Stock Exchange reviewed its computer security, and invited him there to ring the Opening Bell. By the end of the week, Steven had also received commendations from the Mayor, Governor Grassley, and Senator Webster.

The embezzlement story went to the Associated Press service, which distributed it to all its subscribing customers. Hundreds of newspapers around the country had the option of running the story. Many papers in cities around the northeast did just that, including Portland, Springfield, Albany, Scranton and Philadelphia. Newspapers in cities with strong financial institutions also picked it up. Hartford was a double-dip; first being in the same state, and also being home to several major insurance company headquarters, including Aetna, The Hartford and Travelers. Some of those newspapers made inquiries and overtures to Steven about his interest in moving to a bigger city, the same way a college might start recruiting a high school athlete.

Steven was at his desk when his phone rang. It was a call from Hartford. Executives from two insurance companies got together and invited him up for a visit. They were interested in asking him about the case and to learn if there was anything applicable that wasn't in the articles that would help protect their companies and clients. He listened carefully and asked if he could call back in ten minutes. He went into his editor's office to discuss it. They came up with an idea—if the meeting was a two-way street, that is, if he could use his tour of the security of the insurance industry for an article—he'd do it. The headline just about wrote itself. "Is Your Insurance Policy Safe? Did the Banking Scandal Spread to Hartford?" It would be a strong follow-up. He called the executives back and they agreed to his proposal.

He called Susie to tell her he was driving to Hartford the next day. She had been reading the Greenwich and Stamford papers to keep track of what was going on. She and Steven either talked on the phone or saw each other every day. He'd wait for her to ask about the case before he'd say anything, and then he'd always say "she" or "her" instead of using Patty's name. Susie's parents called her once, but they knew their daughters were estranged and that Susie wasn't willing or able to shed more light than what was in the papers. Their local newspaper had joined in the coverage because of Wilton's connection to the story.

Steven had been back in Hartford a few times in the previous couple of years so he still knew his way around. At both companies he received the basic tour and introductory discussion as they strolled around, then continued with coffee and more conversation in a conference room. The executives were a little wary at first but Steven's demeanor and information reassured them their assets and systems were safe as far as he could tell. That would be good news for his readers, and good publicity for the companies. It was a morning well spent.

Steven met some former colleagues for lunch then decided to visit the *Courant* before he drove back to Greenwich. He called ahead so they'd be expecting him. He signed the visitors' log in the front lobby and had no trouble getting in. Some people who remembered him glanced up and waved as he walked through the newsroom. Others came over to say "Hi" and to catch up. He worked his way back to the editor's office to visit the same man who had hired him, then saw him leave a year later.

"Mr. Bowman, great to see you."

"Hi Steven, how are you?"

"Doing well. Thank you for letting me back in here."

"Oh, you're always welcome here, even though you did cause me some trouble."

"How so?"

"You know, your banking embezzlement story on the holiday weekend? My best staff was on vacation. I was scrambling," Bowman said with a smile.

"Sorry about that, Chief," Steven said, imitating Maxwell Smart.

Bowman rolled his eyes. "Same ol' Steven," he said. "Seriously, nice work down there. I wish our paper broke that one."

"Thanks."

The phone rang and Bowman apologized and picked it up. He listened for about fifteen seconds.

"Wait a minute." He covered the mouthpiece with his hand. "I need a couple of minutes for this, okay?"

Steven nodded vigorously and unfolded himself from the seat. He strode out the door then closed it behind him. He leaned against the doorframe and looked over his shoulder, to his right, through the office window and the open Venetian blinds. Bowman turned in his chair, looked at a large map of the state on the wall, and began an animated conversation. Steven decided to stay there rather than wander back into the newsroom. People were working and he had no real business there. He relaxed and waited.

About sixty feet down the hall, past the office window, a door to a conference room opened. Several people streamed out, mostly men in dark suits and shiny black shoes, continuing their conversation in the hallway. It looked like a meeting was taking a break. The group wasn't noisy, but emanated a murmur of a serious tone. It could have been any dozen businessmen in the city, but with one exception—this group contained Mr. Albert D. Flagler.

Steven was certain it was Flagler. He hadn't aged in his forties as much as Steven had grown and filled out in his teens and twenties. Flagler was preoccupied with his group, so Steven had a head start in absorbing what was happening. Soon after, Flagler looked down the hall at the reporter standing outside Bowman's office. It was usually a common sight, but not this time. The reporter was nearly as tall as the doorway, and had recognizable features along with forty extra pounds. Flagler was talking to his associate when it dawned on him who he was looking at. Flagler's associate stopped talking mid-sentence. The

221

associate looked at Flagler, then down the hall at Steven, then back at Flagler before excusing himself and slipping back into the conference room.

Steven watched this minute unfold with a casual yet focused approach. Flagler looked at him as his group drifted apart. Steven pushed off the doorway and pivoted ninety degrees so he was facing squarely down the hall. He stood with his heels slightly wider than shoulder width, slowly folded his arms across his chest, exhaled, and lowered his chin slightly, turning it a bit to the right. Steven unleashed an ice-cold laser beam of a stare and didn't budge.

Flagler was used to being deferred to, and being confident and effective in business situations, in boardrooms and courtrooms. This situation didn't match any of those scenarios. It was probably a complete shock compared to what he was thinking about two minutes earlier. Steven didn't move and didn't let up. Flagler considered several options, but did nothing except squeeze the manila folder he was holding. He rocked forward in his Gucci loafers like he was about to take a step forward then stopped. He started to speak then stopped. Steven didn't move and didn't let up. Flagler broke eye contact first. He looked down at his loafers, then pushed the door and went back into the conference room. Steven tracked him until he was completely out of sight before he budged one inch. He took a deep breath and reached for Bowman's door. It wasn't until later that night that Flagler made the connection and fully understood exactly what had happened. He sat bolt upright in his bed and wanted to talk about it with his wife, but he realized there was no adequate way to explain it to her. He laid back down and stared at the blades of the ceiling fan loop around slowly, and replayed the encounter in his mind over and over until he fell back asleep.

Bowman was off the phone and was looking in his filing cabinet.

"Excuse me again, I have to get back home," Steven said.

Bowman walked over and shook his hand.

"You're always welcome here. I wish I had a half-dozen Stevens out there," he said, turning toward the newsroom.

"Are you kidding? This staff is loaded with Ivy Leaguers."

"Well, keep up the good work," Bowman said.

"Thanks. See you in the papers."

Steven returned his pass in the front lobby and walked to his car parked in a space marked "visitor." This drive from the *Courant* to Greenwich was vastly different than the one in the snow two Februarys earlier. This afternoon the ninety miles seemed like nine. He turned on the radio, found WTIC, and the next song was Foreigner's "Double Vision." This time, he didn't drive home. He went to Susie's house instead.

Chapter Twenty-two

Frank Castino eventually healed enough to stand trial. In the crash on North Street he had suffered a shattered ankle, a broken leg, a ruptured spleen, a broken collarbone, and a concussion. The police investigation yielded new charges including drug and weapons violations, three charges of vehicular manslaughter of his passengers, and two counts of attempted assault of a police officer with a deadly weapon, namely, the speeding Suburban. Police also found a folded Ace of Spades playing card with cocaine residue on it tucked into the visor, and a bag of coke in the glove compartment. A judge quickly agreed the new charges violated Castino's probation, automatically reinstating the convictions and suspended sentences from the Bruce Park Tavern Scandal. For those old convictions, along with these new ones, Castino was sent to the State Prison in Bridgeport for a combination of terms more than long enough to cover the rest of his life. The two other survivors of the crash would join him for forty-year sentences. The three deceased were buried in private, undistinguished ceremonies. Back at Bruce Park Tavern, a spider crawled across the shuffleboard table to reach the cobweb that connected to the wall in the dark, dormant restaurant.

Patty Callahan stood trial on several charges. Her parents attended the trial every day in the Stamford courthouse, but Susie chose not to attend. She had other ways to stay informed. Patty was unanimously convicted by a jury and was sent to the Federal Correction Institution in Danbury, Connecticut.

Ronny Graham was implicated as a co-conspirator, but the case was circumstantial and nothing could be proven beside his financial inattentiveness and negligence, which was actually a result of departmental procedure. Ronny was transferred from Parks & Recreation to the Department of Sanitation, and was assigned to a garbage truck working the alleys behind the Avenue before sunrise. The High School removed his color portrait from its Wall of Fame, as did Mike at the Barber Shop.

Jennifer Johnstone was thoroughly humiliated by both Patty and Ronny. She had no involvement, but her personal dreams came crashing down. She moved to Atlanta where she took a job in the travel department of her father's company. She then struck out on her own, staying in Atlanta, but taking a position with Delta. She became a founding executive in the airline's frequent flier program, and now travels at will, all around the globe.

An independent review found Chief Graham had no knowledge of his brother's or Patty's financial activities. The Chief and the Police Department were lauded for their fine work, which kept their images and reputations intact.

Mark Langford received a special award from Chief Graham and Mayor Bentley for assisting in the capture of a suspected felon. He was honored at one of the morning briefings at the Police Department. Sgt. Heaton was among those who shook his hand. Neither made any mention about their previous meetings along North Street, which magically no longer appeared on his driving record. The YMCA gave him a significant raise and a new title, Vice President of Operations, which enabled and inspired Mark to move into his own place.

In the after-glow of his two big stories, Steven used his short-term power to create some good will and positive spin. He met with Mayor Bentley and Chief Graham and asked that a portion of the Town's money recovered from the Bahamas bank be put to charitable use. He proposed a "Ray Graham/Vietnam Veterans' Children's Fund" to pay for the college educations of children of soldiers Killed-In-Action or Missing-In-Action. The Chief, of course, loved the idea, and the Mayor quickly approved. Steven's only request was that Wendy would be assured a full scholarship to the school of her choice. A photo of the three men shaking hands to announce the new program ran on the front page of the *Greenwich Time*. The day before, he told Susie about it over a candlelight dinner at Manero's. It was a complete surprise and she was thrilled to tears. She said it was the nicest thing anyone had ever done for her.

The door to White's Diner jingled as Steven opened it. He paused for a moment, allowing the warm air to rush into the cool Diner. He was nearly as tall as the doorway, although not nearly as wide, but with his hands on his hips, he filled the frame pretty well. He liked to do that once in a while...sometimes to make a grand entrance, and sometimes just to see what reaction it would get. The Diner was far from a "make a grand entrance" type of place. Instead, the reaction he received was a tilted-head smile from the woman who loved him. Susie stood waiting at his favorite table with a fresh cup of coffee. No cream, no sugar, one ice cube.

Later that fall, Steven sat at his desk in the newsroom. He was admiring a framed photo of himself with Susie and Wendy on vacation in Orlando. Wendy looked happy because Steven had just taught her to do a flip off the diving board. Susie looked happy because their conversations lately contained promises. His phone rang. He drummed a pencil at his desk and looked out the fifth-floor window at the traffic crawling along below him on West Forty-third Street in Manhattan.

"Hello, Steven Rollins, *New York Times*..."

###

About the Author

 **Jim Ramsey** has been writing professionally for nearly thirty years—in newspapers, magazines, television, and books. This is his first novel. Jim grew up in Greenwich, Connecticut, and now lives near Charlotte, North Carolina.

Jim can be contacted through his website, PostRoadPromises.com.

CPSIA information can be obtained at www.ICGtesting.com
Printed in the USA
LVOW01s0429161113

361556LV00005B/442/P